CW01066859

Collected works

Sean Michael Rice

FOREWORD

It was an odd friendship, I suppose, as friendships are usually defined. I can even see where some wouldn't consider it a friendship at all; maybe an acquaintanceship, an ongoing collegial exchange, a professional relationship...but not friends.

I can see their point. In the twenty-two years I knew Sean Michael Rice, we never went out for a drink or a bite to eat, never sat down to shoot the breeze over a cup of coffee. In fact, we were rarely ever in the same room together. Take it one step further: for nineteen of those years, we weren't even in the same state.

Yet when I got the news that Sean had died of lung cancer nine months before, I wept. For days.

I can't explain the connection, only describe it.

12 Miles West was an up-and-coming professional theater company in the tony suburban Jersey town of Montclair. They had started as a ragtag group of theater people performing in a space the local Unitarian Universalist church gave them, then they "graduated" to the upstairs barroom of one of the local saloons, and finally, now fifty members strong, took over a cellar space that had been the site of a failed Mongolian restaurant. They had christened the new space with a one-act festival, and my submission had brought me an invitation to join the company as a resident playwright. There was only one other resident playwright: Sean, who'd been with the company since its first days.

I got my first professional writing gig in 1978: a contract for a screenplay. Since then, of the playwrights, screenwriters, and authors I've met – and the few I've come to know closely – there are only a few I would call true artists. Oh, more than that have thought they were artists, but, for the most part, they've been entertainers and storytellers (giving credit where credit is due, I'd call quite a few of them master storytellers). But artists? Rarely.

To me, that label isn't just about the caliber of the work. There's a sensibility behind the work, a commitment, an almost self-flagellating desire for a perfection of expression that's probably not attainable, and whose unattainability is the artist's white whale; beckoning him/her onward, always out of reach, generating creative ambition and creative dissatisfaction simultaneously.

Put another way, artists go where other creatives can't...or won't. Put still another way: artists can't stop themselves from going where other creatives can't...or won't.

Sean Michael Rice was, in my eyes, as pure a literary artist as I've ever known. That he considered me a peer, a colleague, an equal let alone a friend, is an accolade that, to this day, I find mystifying because I never once, even in my most vain moments, ever considered myself remotely in his league.

We didn't spend a lot of time together in the few years we were both at 12MW. I had a fulltime job in New York and the only hours I could spend at the theater were contributed work hours on weekends, sometimes working the house during a show, and, of course, whenever one of my handful of pieces was being presented. But whenever I saw Sean, he was quick to come up, take my hand or clap me on the back to congratulate me on whatever short piece had recently been up, to talk it up as some impressive piece of stage work; attention I felt it hardly warranted.

I was at the company meeting (a story related later in this collection) where Sean exploded over the company's distractions with property maintenance, appeasing bruised egos, and sundry other topics for bickering and pissing and moaning. As I watched Sean storm out of that meeting, I shrank a little in my seat feeling like I was a pretender just being in the room with him after seeing how much he cared.

I'm not a theater guy. I'd always felt I was at the company on a pass. I'd stumbled into writing for the stage, the one-act which had gotten me my invitation having only been written because a friend of mine had asked for a short piece for a play reading group he was trying to launch. And here I was surrounded by people who'd, for some years, dedicated themselves heart and soul to the art and craft of the stage, and none of them seemed as purely invested in heart and soul as Sean.

Bluntly, Sean didn't give a shit about anything other than – his frequent words – The Work. If it would have focused the company more acutely on The Work, Sean would've been happy mounting his stuff in an empty lot.

Proof: When I asked Sean for a piece about his writing for a book I was doing about people in the arts, he only agreed as a favor, convinced he had little worthwhile to offer (it's included later in this volume). In that piece was the first time I had any idea of what Sean had done as an actor and writer since he'd never talked about it. In 2017, when I first approached him about the possibility of putting his short fiction and poetry together as a collection for publication, he poo-pooed the idea thinking nobody could possibly be interested enough in his work to publish it. The only way I got him to agree was by begging and offering to put his work into manuscript form for him since Sean saved no digital versions of his work (when he finally sent me his material, it came as a bundle of Xeroxes and hand-written stuff on scraps of paper).

Sometime around 1998, 12 Miles West fell into a sort of civil war between various factions. Don't ask me to explain it as I never quite understood it other than as a tragically avoidable confluence of egos, unrealistic expectations, and petty gripes. Fed up, Sean left the company. I stuck it out a bit longer, but when I saw, despite one turnover among the top echelon, that things weren't going to get any better, I bailed as well.

I can't recall how the correspondence between Sean and me got started. All I remember is that he left Jersey and wound up on a mountaintop farm somewhere in Pennsylvania and that for nearly two decades, he and I exchanged letters. Not emails; good old-fashioned letters which, from Sean, were often still handwritten when they weren't being written on "the old typer."

Some of it was chit-chat; him talking about tooling around the fields on the farm's tractor, motorcycling around Pennsylvania's back roads, and me talking about my work at HBO, my marriage, my kids. Sometimes we traded movie trivia. Sean would come across an article he thought I might be interested in and send it along; I sent him Lee Server's biography of Robert Mitchum because we were both fans. And, of course, we kept each other up on our writing. Once we were both tickled that we had pieces up on the same one-act slate at a black box in New York ("Butch and Sundance together again!" I wrote him sending him a copy of the night's program), and I was equally tickled to write to him afterward about how well his piece had gone over. Every time each of us had a piece up somewhere – a New York black box, a school auditorium out in the Jersey boonies, a bit of prose in a small, nearly invisible literary magazine – we'd celebrate and salute the other, because to Sean, any time "The Words" got "out there," it was a victory.

Letter by letter, we grew closer than we had at the theater. He always asked about my kids, even sent them picture books he'd found at a local flea market, and I asked about his life on the farm. Maybe we weren't friends the way most people think of friendship. Maybe it was more like a Band of Brothers thing. But after twenty-odd years, the bond was there, and it was a strong one, stronger than a bull session over coffee or a drink could ever have produced.

I had wondered why his letters had become more sporadic and it was only later, when I'd learned he'd been fighting cancer for his last two-and-a-half years that I understood. Sean had never mentioned his illness.

The way I found out he had passed was like this:

After a year or so of trying, in the early part of 2018, I'd finally found a home for his book of short works and poems. I tried the email he used only sporadically but it had been discontinued. I wrote to tell him the good news and instruct him to get in touch with the publisher; papers were going to have to be signed, some editorial consultation done. No answer. I wrote again, pushing him to get moving. Again, no answer. I thought perhaps he'd moved or was off on one of his road trips. I finally wrote addressing the letter:

Sean Michael Rice

(or anybody who knows Sean)

The daughter of the family who owned the farm, and who, apparently, had become quite close with Sean over the years, considering him family, wrote to tell me that Sean had died the previous June.

I was later told by a cousin of his that in the years Sean was being treated for his cancer, he never complained. He'd wanted to die at home with his cats, and when the cousin had gone to pick Sean up for a doctor's appointment, she'd discovered that was exactly how he had passed.

I was also told she'd found my letters among his things. I suppose that says something about our tie since I still have all the letters he'd written me.

Back in our 12MW days, I'd suspected Sean was a damaged soul, scarred by a war uglier than most. It's all through his work. But he'd seemed to find some kind of peace on that mountaintop farm. At least I hope he did. It had been another hope of mine that perhaps he would find some -- ... I don't know; solace, resolution, closure to see his works, many of which are woven through with his demons and unhealed wounds, published in a single volume. It will always haunt me that he didn't get to see this book come to be.

The day he passed, I took myself to one of the local saloons – the kind of place Sean would've felt at home in – and bought myself a rare drink to toast my friend.

Maybe, when you're done with this book, you'd oblige me by doing the same.

Bill Mesce, Jr.
Farmington, ME
3/18

Table of Contents

Collected Works

GONE

—Somewhere in the framework of time without any warning
swept from earth. Never to take another breath. Forever gone.

soaring on the warm wind

over crawling cold waters,

striving to be everywhere at once

on my solitary wandering.

halting the dreaming about life & just plain livin' it,

an unfolding flow

within the daily pattern of life where I watch

the strength of my good-hearted spirit falls away

from time as I haunt like a floating ghost on the

rainy twilight eve of night.

movin' easy down the line to a silent hideaway

among the shadows forgetting what I don't want

to remember as I drift on a fresh river flow under

the blessed sky.

WINTERS PAST

Remember those winters mornings
when early we did rise,
and I dressed
and rode away
in that winter haze;
the week it was of lonely
my thoughts just of you
but once again on Friday
we embraced
when in sight,
and all that rifle firing
was lost
to a winter night.

PASSING THROUGH

—for days now i've been driving Mom around the territory.

crossing borders, traveling to the heartland.

catching up with the brilliant disguise of

        season brushed colors.

a dreamscape of peace within the feel of rain.

days into nights of golden-red sunsets & blazing layered clouds

        layered clouds of awakening skies.

moving further, further down the line to the

        faraway of everywhere.

all the way along the winding highway Mom's ashes

        soaring gracefully forever.

on the mercy of heavenly flight.

MOJAVE

Road lines flashing. Thoughts quick shining shadowland images Brother Duke to Vietnam. 14 days later killed by rocket fire. I touch out to his name on the shiny black Vietnam Memorial.

Crippled tortured thoughts.

Brother Barry who on June starry night blew himself away.

Quick shining nothing is forever thoughts.

Dad's cancer-ravaged body ravaged mumbling incoherent tunnel words. Mom one year later passing in the silent night.

Road lines hold me captive.

On either side of the road CLOSED signs. American ruins beat by the passage of time. Eyes to the rearview I'm surrounded by the naked limbs of cemetery trees.

"What do I have to lose," I whisper to the headlight glow that slashes the darkness, "nothing is forever."

I turn the Chevy pickup onto old Route 66. West to the red dawn.

½ day later.

Mojave Desert. Wool blanket heat. Joshua trees in inspirational postured reverence corral O.J. Simpson posed on a rock.

3 hours earlier

Los Angeles

Watching O.J. and his golf buddies laughing back slapping. Shameless. Enjoying life with a killer…

Eyes rooted on O.J. as he carried his clubs to his shiny car.

O.J. loading the trunk. I asked for an autograph.

"Absolutely," O.J. turned smiling only to be met with a 5-1/2" barrel 6-shooter in my right leather gloved hand.

"Lessgo." I hustled O.J. into my pickup. Snapped on handcuffs.

Route 15 north

Mojave silence

"Birds lizards insects depend upon the Joshua tree. Ecosystem. You'd think the Joshua's are praying arms raised like they are to the heavens."

"You joking with O.J.?"

"How do you like my gun? Classic western look. Caliber .357 magnum. Most advanced single-action revolver ever produced."

"Stop joking with O.J. This is crazy."

"Yeh." I raised the polished stainless-steel barrel, "You killed Nicole and Ron Goldman."

"I never..."

I waved the shiny barrel like a naughty finger, "Truth."

"Never killed..."

Trigger pulled. Pin down against the cap. Speeding bullet.

O.J.'s right foot flesh blood bone became one with the Mojave.

"This revolver delivers superb accuracy with very mild recoil. Helluva firearm don't you think?"

Ignoring me, O.J. pierced the Mojave with a screaming cry.

"Truth."

O.J. turned his arrogant face to me, "Didn't kill..."

Trigger finger .357 discharged. Left foot smashed. O.J. caved to the Mojave floor. Blinding hot scream.

"Bet you wish now you were locked away for your killings."

O.J. cursing pain, "I'm defenseless...helpless."

I almost laughed but it was too damn pitiful, "Like Nicole and Ron?"

"You crazy?"

16

"Yeh." Revolver sighted. "You killed..."

"Didn't..."

Trigger freed. O.J.'s left knee shattered. Scream covered Mojave.

"Looks like no more golf for you."

O.J. lost in his wail.

"Nicole and Ron are silent...forever."

Even in his hellish pain O.J. tried to stare me down. Cold-Blooded.

.357 cocked. O.J. swallowed. Mercy within. I eased the sturdy hammer. O.J. let go a steamed breath. Revolver holstered in back pocket. I heaved that blood load back onto the rock. Knife from jacket pocket. Glistening sharp.

Bugging eyed O.J. "I did it." I went behind O.J. his big head flagged, "I did it." Couldn't stop himself now. Slashing images of that bloody Brentwood night I guess. "Did it...did..."

I held the blade to O.J.'s neck as I unlocked the cuffs. His arms flopped down like a puppet. O.J. put his hands to his blood parts. I gave him a rag for the blood, "Wipe your hands." I housed pocketed the blade. Gripping the revolver, "Write what I tell you."

O.J. looked up to face an aged folded piece of paper partnered with a pencil looped in a stringed hangman's noose jailed on a clipboard. O.J. took the clipboard and pencil in his shaky hands.

"On the top fold write, I AM BEING MADE TO WRITE THIS AT GUN POINT."

O.J. slowly worked the pencil, "I'm bleeding aparts."

"When you're finished I'll bandage you doctor like. Now on the bottom fold write, I KILLED NICOLE AND RON GOLDMAN. I AM TRULY SORRY. SORRY."

"I won't write that."

I put the .357 to his good knee. "I KILLED..." O.J. wrote.

17

"Now add, I PRAY TO GOD TO FORGIVE ME FOR KILLING TWO DEFENSELESS HELPLESS PEOPLE."

O.J. hesitated then eyed that mighty gun.

"Autograph. Date it June 6, 1996."

"It's 2001."

I nudged his knee with the shiny barrel. O.J. wrote. I took up the confession, "Justice."

"There is no justice."

"Old west kind."

Under O.J.'s breath, "He wasn't that helpless."

"Say again."

Arrogant faced silence.

A fly landed on my right arm. Holding the revolver steady I flashed my left hand. Opening my fingers I peeked the fly crawling on the tight leather. "Over there's your diner." The two-wings rushed to O.J.'s red.

"I'm gonna bleed to death."

"Like you let Nicole and Ron..."

"Didn't kill..."

"Spin on it." Hammer freed. O.J.'s right hand mangled. Off he fell from the rock. Fainted away. I wrapped O.J.'s wounds so he wouldn't bleed to death. Wanted O.J. alive to face each day without his precious golf. Wall staring for O.J. Harvesting water and a large red beach umbrella from the bed of the pickup I went to O.J. planted the water by his good hand then stuck the umbrella into the Mojave to shade O.J. from the banking sun.

Framed Mojave still life.

O.J. half-closed eyes. "You won't get away with this."

"Nothing is forever."

"Huh?"

"When I'm down the road a few I'll let the powers that be know where they can find you. Won't be hard to miss this red umbrella. Shouldn't be an hour."

I looked to the praying Joshua trees then to no good O.J.

"Guess you wouldn't tell me what you did with the killing knife."

Arrogant faced O.J.

I raised the polished stainless-steel barrel, "High noon showdown."

O.J. gulped that hot Mojave air.

I lowered the classic western revolver, "Just kidding." I went to the pickup and was about to get in when I turned with the confession, "Truth."

O.J. framed in arrogance, "Useless. Worthless."

The confession escapes the clipboard, "See how it's folded smart guy. Gun threat...top fold. Confession signature date...bottom. Just tear away top fold...truth."

"Double jeopardy. Can't get me for doing it."

"I did."

Wrote at gun point."

"Don't forget dated 1996. No gun pointed at you in '96. So I'm betting you don't say jack about me or the direction I'm headed. By any chance I lose that bet...be as famous as you. Get a bit of the spotlight. And that's one thing for certain I can bet. The O.J. wouldn't want to share his shine. Then again should I get the lockup..." I waved the confession to the Joshua trees.

"You're a no good killer, O.J."

"You're no better. Slaughtering me likes this. No better."

"One day we'll face the heavenly justice. Know that. Then we'll see, O.J. We will see."

Mojave silence.

I got into the pickup, "Look out for vultures."

O.J.'s frantic eyes to the cobalt sky.

I drive east.

9 hours later

A hard rain falling on old Route 66.

8-1/2 hours since I called the powers and told them where to find
O.J.

Eyes to the rearview. Lost in a harvest moon glow. Surrounded by
the naked limbs of cemetery trees. Carved deep on a gray tombstone

NOTHING IS FOREVER

rain slashes at the headlight glow

i drive the wet blacktop

DISTANCE

early red morning sky.
heading outta this gutter hot town before another day
dies.

v a m o o s e

gas pedal punch & i'm across the dusty border to a
forest green village.

clean & sweet in the air.

no boarded up, closed down, paint peeling houses.

no rusty autos perched atop cinder blocks on grass
dried dead.

red dresses & blue jeans swing dance on sunny white
lines.

man O, man, getting a deep breath of fresh mowed
hay.
        Driving west under heaven burnt clouds,
steering a subterranean path to the weathered map in
my head.

dying light surrenders to a brilliant harvest moon
disguise.

Yellow road lines stream past broken hearted
dreams, as the starry night fades behind dark clouds.

On the midnight horizon a splintered charging
spirit glow.

Down the old road the syncopating beat of rainy
Wipers.

Two-lanes of blacktop lift out of the sharp
daybreak shadows, the ribbon of snaking road hightails
across the great American landscape.

black coffee & cheeseburgers at roadside diners.
hide-away the nights at lumpy mattress motels.
gas, oil, Coke bottle from the machine.

Clouds sweep the countryside, spreading wave
Upon wave of sideway sliding shadows.

A caboose disappears down the high noon tracks.

Miles ahead a crossroad sign post, a buffalo
head flip steers my destiny.

eyes to the rearview.

surrounded by naked limbs of cemetery trees.

a lone soul kneels in prayer by a blackening tombstone,
chiseled deep

N O T H I N G   I S   F O R E V E R

Drumming a steady tempo on the sturdy wheel
that guides the tires flow to yet another direction of
escape.
Around a long sweeping curve, end of the day
golden drenched holy light rains a salvation of
heartworn yesterdays.

DRIVE

Behind the wheel.
Red '55 Chevy.
283 engine with 2-4 barrels.
 3-speed on the column.

Clear road ahead. Fly. Puttin' that dirty gutter hot town behind me before another day dies. Outta town past weather beaten road signs. To the windshield comes the morning light. Sharp shadows. The road dust stirs. The tires rush the baking blacktop. Nice & easy the Chevy passes a plastic motel, "Hey I can see you in there makin' time." Her stockings and underthings hang over a chair. The floor is a bundle of polyester and cotton. The sheets are steamin' with sweat (nice & easy does it). A light punch on the gas and I'm into a fresh community. Clean & sweet in the air. No fire escapes. No cigarette ads with women showin' off their long silky legs. Bright colors dance on clothes lines in that clean & sweet. Take a deep breath. Now is the time. Breath. Dream. Gatherin' speed. Drivin' west through the late afternoon. The shadows lengthen. Then the dark and the glow of the moon. An hour down the road the moonlight disappears behind the westward map in my head. In between Elvis and Johnny Cash I get the time. In between Chuck Berry and Ricky Nelson, I get the newsflash. I'm in the fast lane. The radio is at full blast and I drive. I cut between cars & trucks. I don't need the brake I'm good enough with the clutch. Playin' the gears. I travel the road west. Black coffee and cheese burgers at small roadside diners. Hide-away the nights at small roadside motels. Ice machine OUT OF ORDER. Hot. Gettin' hotter. Day into night. Watchin' blurry visions on black&white television in small hot rooms. Lump mattress sleep.

"You wasted all my good years," I looked up and around, caught hold of April's eyes in the rearview, "nothing came of our life together," April's lips move in slow motion.

"No, we had fun," I was about to say, but then April's eyes were lost to the mirrored glass. I woke two hours later. Blurry visions. Yeah, that's it. I started the engine, eased the red '55 onto the early morning blacktop. Rollin' on. Movin' on across the territory. Gettin' away from things. Everyday different. But then at times there's no change. It all just begins to look the same.

Drivin' smooth & easy on Route 66, when this '59 Cadillac Coupe de Ville, the one with the bomber tail lights...Man O, man, it flies by me like I'm standin' still. I double clutch and scoot that lever to 2nd. Put the pedal to the floor, power shift into 3rd and that '55 Chevy WHOA it damn near jumped into the other lane. That baby ScReaMed after that Caddy's tail. For the next 100 miles we chased each other across the western plains. The late afternoon sun hot off the hood and under the visor. It got so I could barely see past the blaze of light. Squintin' tight. Then we came to these dark rolling hills of blacktop. Caddy on the crest, Chevy in the valley. Yeah, man O, man turned into darkness FREED into light. FLY. Engine oil sizzlin'. Tires burnin'. Roll MoNsTeR machine, roll. Yeh man, yeh, into that vicinity of GO.

Then the '55 sputtered back. The Caddy blazed ahead kickin' up a cloud of dust. The tail lights were lost from sight. And the sun goes down alone. Burnin' red dyin' into the horizon.

Gas.

Water.

Oil.

Coke bottle from the machine.

Drive. Lost within that vicinity of go. I got this pain in my chest. I parked the Chevy in the desert under a billion stars. A coffin of silence. If I die now, ok...into DrEaMs I drive...EXIT awake with the red sun...pain gone. Alive&kickin'. The '55 in the eastward lane of Route 66. Drive. Go straight through the days. Chevy curbside. Tired. So tired. I just sat there as minutes died. After Buddy Holly's last lick, I got out of the Chevy. Polished a spot off the hood, then went up the walkway. Jumped the 3 steps onto the porch. Rang the bell. Could see movement through the window. Nobody answered. Knocked against the window with a buffalo head nickel. That did it. The door opened. He wasn't lookin' too happy seein' me there. Didn't think I was a good influence on his daughter.

"April doesn't want to see you anymore."

That can't be. No, it couldn't be too late. Me and April had the same heartbeat. I spotted April in the shadows by the kitchen doorway, "Love you." He pushed me. I almost fell down the steps. I could've hurt myself fallin' off that porch. I didn't want to be unpleasant. He didn't understand and I told him so.

"Dumb, young and full of it," he yawned at me.

I tried to get past him. Had to get to April. Tell her about being parked under those billion stars. Beautiful peace. He gave me another push. Harder than the last. I stumbled back, fell down the steps. Jeans torn. Knee scraped. I put my hand to the blood and looked up at him. He shook his head and laughed. Turned his back on me. Was just closin' the door when I yelled, "Hey." He spun around his fists clenched. I pulled back my coat. Showed him the Colt .45 that was holstered between my belt and jeans, "Draw."

Then again, "Dumb, young and full of it."

I drew the Colt. Pulled back the hammer. Looks like he's goin' for his gun. That 6-shooter deep in his holster. He's gonna fan it. I gently freed the fresh trigger. No more pushin' meanness. The mother was rushin' down from the 2nd floor. I raised the Colt. Reflex action. Didn't mean to do her. She wasn't a bad one. Then the brother came barrelin' up from the basement. Thought I saw somethin' shiny. 2 bullets did that big strapper.

April was balled up in the corner of the kitchen cryin'.

"Lessgo." We hadda get outta town. Yeh, past those weather-beaten road signs. Drive. April didn't move. I thought she loved me. Cared. We had nice drives. We'd watch the sun go down.

I got some chocolate milk from the ice-box. Poured out a full glass. Was gonna drink it from the bottle, then thought better of it. Not too healthy. April was still cryin'. Sounded like a child lost in a dark dream of night.

somehow
someway

I could hear my daddy screamin' at my mom, "Shut that kid up. Shut him!" I kept on cryin'. Must've sounded pretty much like April. I would've never yelled for my child to shut up. I'd come into the room, "Hush now, hush." Or sing a soft song. A peaceful song that would put the child to sleep under the billion stars of night. Gentle sleep.

I cocked the Colt. No more nightmares. Never have to grow-up. Just like in Peter Pan. Fly. Drive. Gettin' lost in that coffin of silence.

But then ever so slowly I released the burnin' hammer. Slow. Gentle. I put the Colt atop the ice-box. Didn't want it to get into the hands of any children. Might hurt themselves.

Gently I held April, "Hush now...hush," and began to sing a peaceful song. Softly. Tenderly. And I knew then and there that once upon a time I almost had it made

asleep in the desert
under a billion stars

RELATIONSHIP

She straddled me & said

she loved me

A few seconds later

she cursed me for my 2 day growth of beard

I told her a bill collector called

she screamed not to tell her what to do

I pushed her off & got a beer

"What's wrong?" she asked

I finished that beer & had another

"Let's talk" she said

I had enough of talk

I had another beer & turned on the TV

the baseball game was boring, but the commercials

not ½ bad.

(She has since locked herself into the bathroom,

I guess she doesn't love me anymore)

WRITER

i hold the Bic pen to the hot bulb of naked light-
been checking' the level of ink on the daily-
would've thought after all i've written
the ink would've gone down a bit-
but i have yet to see any sign-

faster & harder with the Bic-
layin' down letters
fightin' em into words
battlin' the ink hard & fast
by the naked bulb of light-
Man-O-man the time is a-flashin'
as i'm warehouse stackin' the sheets of white-
that someone, someday
might come to read-
but if they don't that's OK
bottom line i write 1st for me-

as the Bic scrambles by the bulb's naked red-hot light
i'm outta the corner to fight the good fight-
yeah, i'm here to tell ya
the ink is gonna go down
tonight.

FLOW

At an intersection in the East Village a stocky man with a battered face jacks open the door to my taxi his pudgy bruised hand grips a Smith & Wesson .38. the instant before the bluish barrel burrows hard into my temple I see myself smiling on a children's swing Sailing way up high to the heavenly clouds A far away voice whispers, "Look to the moon on lost nights see me in its brilliant light" Reaching for the glorified shine I fall from the swing into a deep dark tunnel where there comes an explosion that slams my head against the window Blood pours from the fleshy bone exit Red slowly snakes down the window Eyes are dead-set blue on the windshield The taxi jumps the curb and drifts across a deserted lot where it comes to rest against a pile of bricks and rubble Through the afternoon the taxi idles under the hot boil of August At dusk the last drop of gas flows through the carburetor The engine sputters then comes the still coffin silence inside the taxi as the air conditioner gives up its last breath of cold

I move restless under the covers trying to go back to my deadly nightmare. Want to see what happens next. Was not a good sleep that's for sure. Hopefully that framework isn't a stirring for what lays down the line. "Man, I own this here city. Drive where I please." Kicking back the covers in a mad fury I go to the bathroom mirror, "Mornin' brother, how y'be?"

After downing a black coffee, I make my way down the broken steps to the broken street. I look to the top of the building, at least there's a blue sky for me this day.

Shuffling along West 47th Street I whistle a Dylan song from the sixties. Believe it's Lay Lady, Lay. Yeah, think that's the one. But maybe not. My head is wrapped funny strange these days. But then sidewinding around

31

the corner I know for sure that I'm whistling Subterranean Homesick Blues, a hard-whistling tune to be sure, but I'm hitting the notes.

Then I think about her. Yeah, good solid thoughts as I take on the next couple blocks. She was a good one. Let her slip away. Crazy. Yeah, I could be so crazy and nuts. Then I hear her say, "I'm sorry now I spent all those years with you. Wasted years. I lost sight of myself because of you."

"Yeah, what the hell blame me. What does it matter? Doesn't matter anymore. All I ever wanted was for you to value your life. You had it so good from the very beginning and never appreciated it. Took it all for granted."

"Like you took me."

"I didn't mean to."

"But you did."

"Guess we all do. Human nature, eh? But bottom line no matter what, I still love you."

"I don't love you. Not anymore. And I loved you so much. You were everything to me."

"Rainy Day Women."

"What?"

"The Dylan song, y'know?"

"You give me the title of a song after what I just said."

"Well, y'know..."

"No, I don't know. You're hopeless."

"Remember when..."

"When what?"

"Well...how I used to make you happy."

"Happy?"

"Yeah, y'know, once upon a time."

"Hopeless."

At Rudy's Bar & Grill I catch sight of me in the mirrored window. Moving up close I try to spy what's deep down in these here eyes, "Gimme an answer." Blink. "That's it, huh?" Shrugging I walk south on 9th Avenue stumbling off the cracked curb I did up Lay Lady, Lay once again. This time I'm right on the money and out comes a clear strong whistle. Even get myself a smile from a lovely wearing a short denim skirt. Must be a dancer what with those shapely beauties.

After a few hours of worthwhile fares, I park by an old Bowery diner. Sitting over a cup of black coffee I put pen to napkin:

Out of the corner of my eye I catch sight of a pretty girl in a '57 Chevy with bare feet up on the dashboard. I slow and check the girl-next-door beauty. "Man, there was a time once" I mumble to the rearview flowery dress. "A long ago once upon a time."

Slant ink, drain black:

Drove out of town on a one-way street on the wettest day of the year. Was escaping a large L-shaped room that was walled with photos of a beautiful woman. Across the borderline I turned onto a straight-ahead road. Was bound and determined to drive that blessed day into a sacred night without stopping. As the sky burned I softly sang an old gospel to the rearview, "When I learned enough to really live, I'll be old enough to die."

I stare out the soiled window at the passing parade of folks trying to do their best in this here life. "Yeah, maybe I am hopeless," I mumble to the window. "What the hell regret is just a scrambled memory, ain't a thing I can do about it now."

Sliding behind the wheel I hear myself whistling Like A Rolling Stone. Then I look to the rearview and smile, "I ain't countin' y'out brother. Nope, not yet."

33

Then it's forward ahead back into the framework of NYCity life

subways cursing the underground
jackhammers pounding,
horns blaring,
neon blues fill the steel frames.
jazz, rock 'n' roll, classical strings ride the
waves for all the lost wandering souls, who
slow dance through swirling steamy clouds
that rise ghostly from the rumbling bowels
of Manhattan.

Freewheelin' positively south on Lafrayette past the Public Theater, it's a TRACERS reigning marquee. "Peace, good brothers…peace."

My thoughts race on the long and winding to my good buddy Duke. #1 outstanding recruit of his platoon. Duke wrote his family that even after all the training, what he had learned, been told, nothing truly prepared him for what Vietnam was really like. Duke was killed by enemy rocket fire while in patrol in Quang Nam Province, 5May'68. He was in Nam less than two weeks. 21 years old. Duke's flag covered coffin came home to rest under Arlington soil.

"You would've dug Tracers Duke. A kaleidoscopic trip through the wilds of Nam with the warriors assaulting all the senses. Yeah, you'd dig. Bless ya brother."

On the upper West Side at 79th & Riverside Drive a mighty whirlwind blows a clear view of the fast-flowing Hudson. It's there by Riverside Park that I roll to a stop, pull out my notebook and spill out on the page

—somewhere in the framework of time without any

Warning swept from earth

        —never to take another breath-forever gone

—SCREAM your head off, let go.
—SCREAM like you've never
screamed, blow y'all, blow
—SCREAM your head, let blow-whoa
man,
—WHOA, slam them brakes before you crash the pearly
gates
—LIVE

    Traveling on a spirited curve on a quick night of life's rhyme I rescue a tall tailored beauty from a windy East Side corner. Pulling a U-turn, I head northward. Driving on the smooth I come across Kitchman's hap cab shuffle, a quick salute, then it's forward ahead on the go delivering the perfumed curves to a midnight paradise, where orchids are glory white under the moon's glow.

ROAD DrEaM

sometimes on that off night

i lay down & sleep easy

then i dream

  on the road into the dream i drive

clear path ahead =into curves =passin' shadows

& there's no stoppin' me as i drum that steerin' wheel

Yeh, keepin' right up with that

rock&roll&rhythm&blues

& then comes a heavy blink of the lids,

i look up&about LosT in a buried room

Of dark CrAcKeD shadowed corners,

    Route 66 nowhere in sight

yeh, the drive is in the dream,

& then i ImaginE

In that dreamy drvin' dark

it best to be

  The Lone Ranger

on the road= everyday different= passin' through=new directions=

tryin' to do the good

  in the wild seed territory,

i squeeze behind the wheel of my mighty steed

slam the pedal to the floor

rearin-up in a cloud of dust i give out a hearty

    "Hi Yo Silver"

  racin' across the Mojave

coyotes HOWL as clouds unmask a ghostly moon,

i spur on my fiery steed across the western plains

through the canyons= down the pass= onto Route 66

& the road lines f= L= o= W=

past broken shadowed dreams

past weathered&battered structures

American ruins CLOSED

yeh, how those road lines f =L =o =W =

past the good&bad scrambled-up

  in the vanishing landscape,

dreamin' on the drive, or drivin' within a dream

i tear off the mask

        &

into the dark CRaCkeD shadowed corners

        i drive= = = =

SUDDENLY

buried in cold dreams

nesting among show shawled limbs,

then slowly awake to the home warmth of morning light.

waiting — hoping

that the snowy streets will keep me homebound,

sledding, snowballs, digging tunnel deep in the cold white.

tunneling to a frozen hideaway

where the wind sweeps over

icy fields to the far other side

where I sit in the shelter

of northern winter light.

imaging those youthful long ago snowy days,

a sudden passage of bundled wintry time,

when I blended with the white landscape.

JULY 29th, 1890

under the burning Auvers sky

the pained hand of suffering

touches the brush

to the rich wet color,

the red-bearded man strokes

a grand passionate sweep across the canvas,

a lush gold, shaded with a trace of green,

a strong stroke follows,

the gold-green is host

to a brilliant sun-filled blue,

an encompassing blue

that blesses the canvas in truth,

breathing softly the man captures

with beauty and peace

the full glory of nature,

the red-bearded man touches the brush

to a ripe golden-yellow,

as the brush is freed upon the canvas

a spreading breeze caresses

the pastures of heaven.

I AM NOT DEAD, I SENT THIS
POSTCARD FROM HELL

I met Barry Brown at the Los Angeles theatre the spring of 1976 when we were cast in the World Premier of Tina Howe's Museum. Among the Company: Ralph Waite, Dana Elcar, Diane White, Bill Bushnell, Betty Aberlin, Fox Harris, Ron Rickards, and Philip Baker Hall.

Barry approached me at the end of the first week of rehearsal holding a switchblade, "Thought this would work for your character," he laughed.

"Appreciate, but, I'm thinking more subtle."

"Subtle?"

"Choices, y'know?"

"Hear that."

A week later I was having a beer at Vera Cruz, a down and out bar around the corner from the theatre on Santa Monica Boulevard. Barry settled on the neighboring stool, "Choices," he laughed, then ordered a whiskey, "The play seems to be coming together."

"Dana Elcar's a terrific director."

"Dana's one of the good ones in this town. What's your history?"

"My lady Nancy and I arrived in LA back in February by train after five years in Manhattan."

"Train?"

"Came the southern route. Had a helluva overnight in New Orleans."

"What did you do in New York?"

"Actors Studio. Off-Off Broadway. Motorcycle messenger. Had two of my plays produced at the New York Theatre Ensemble."

"I had a one-act produced last year."

"Yeah?"

"Not New York."

"Hey man, it was just Off-Off Broadway."

"Still."

"Yeah, it was a kick."

"I've been wanting to get myself to New York, just can't seem to escape LA. Can I read some of your stuff?"

"If I can read yours."

"You got it."

I raised my beer to the smoky ceiling, "To theatre."

Friendship born.

AUGUST 1977

A packed audience in a large theatre space behind an old book store on Vermont Avenue. Philip Baker Hall and I did a kick ass staged reading of my play When Bogart Was. Barry was raving with enthusiasm in the corner. You'd think it was a sport event what with his cheering. It was a stirring night. Even so that Philip and I were given the go ahead to have Bogart produced at the Los Angeles Actors Theatre.

After the reading Barry joined Nancy and me at our Beachwood Canyon apartment to share a few ounces. Barry proved from our times spent at the Vera Cruz that he could put away a steady flow. At our place on the heavy-duty nights he'd crash on our couch. First thing in the morning Barry would pour himself a tall something or other.

A few months later the drink began to cause erratic behavior. Auditions were blown. Every now and again Barry tried to stop. Gave it a good fight. It was at these times that Barry gave a backward glance. A patchwork of words made up of ifs, ands, and buts. In 1972, Barry co-starred with Jeff Bridges in Robert Benton's Bad Company.

In his stir of words Barry quickly passed over a failed marriage, "We went wrong fast." We didn't look on the bright side of life. "My biggest regret was losing out on the part of Tod Hackett in Nathaneal West's The Day of the Locust. Had a number of meetings with John Schlesinger at the Bel Air Hotel. One delay after another. I really wanted that one. In '73 director Peter Bogdanovich offered me the part of Frederick Winterbourne in Daisy Miller. Bogdanovich had scored big time with The Last Picture Show so I had high hopes for Daisy, especially since it starred his girlfriend Cybill Shepherd. Tangled experience."

Then smiling broadly, "The high point of the whole deal for me was when Elizabeth Taylor stopped by our set in Rome. I pulled her aside and did my Montgomery Clift impression. I knew that they had been great friends and thought she'd get a kick. And fortunately, she did. When I returned from Rome my agent got me this action movie Ultimate Thrill. Man, disaster."

With the exception of Disappearance of Aimee with Bette Davis, Barry was pretty much on a dry streak. The high ground of the critically acclaimed Bad Company was a dusty memory. At the age of 26, Barry was looking to make a comeback.

EARLY JUNE 1978

"I'm going away," Barry smiled.

"Where to?"

"No," choking a laugh, "I mean I'm going away...gonna kill myself."

Through the stretching darkness we talked of life, death, the whole damn deal.

Barry's sense of humor always at hand, joked later that night about ways of doing it. One of which was driving his Volkswagen Beetle off Mulholland Drive in front of Brando's house. Dawn came with Barry smiling, "If I don't do it in the next two weeks...I won't do it."

Barry vanished into the summer smog. There was no getting in touch. A few days short of the second week a very serene Barry was at our door. "I'm moving out to Silver Lake. Had enough of that old paint peeling Victorian. Started moving into a downtown apartment."

Fifteen minutes later we're standing in a clean compact apartment. A good many of his books were piled next to his electric typewriter. Poster of Bad Company was hanging high on the fresh painted wall. After toasting his new digs with green barreled bottles of Mickeys, Barry took me out to lunch at Musso & Frank. Whenever we scored jobs we'd celebrate at Hollywood's oldest restaurant, which in its heyday was the haunt of F. Scott Fitzgerald, Dashiell Hammet, and Raymond Chandler.

Barry raised his glass, "To a celebration of new beginnings."

An hour later as we were getting ready to leave, Barry smiled a broad smile, then coughed up a mighty laugh, "Forget that talk I talked. The best is yet to come."

JUNE 27th

After a day's shoot on Roots: The Next Generation at Union Station, I motorcycled north on the Hollywood Freeway. On a flashing thought that Barry might still be moving from the Victorian I took the Silver Lake exit. Rolling down Mohawk Avenue I saw his battered green Volks parked in the driveway.

Parking behind the Beetle I spied Barry's stereo in the front seat. Up on the creaky porch I knocked on the shaky door.

Silence.

On impulse I went around back, up the wooden stairs, and through the broken screen door. It was the route I always took when I looked after his shaggy black dog Goofy.

I walked across the hot empty top floor, "Yo Barry." Downstairs. Boxes, magazines, newspapers, scattered. In the shadows of the dining room I saw Barry dressed in T-shirt and jeans stretched out on the mattress.

From where I was standing the coating of deep shadows etched Barry's face as a horror mask. Slowly a revolver came into focus on the right edge of the mattress.

After calling the police, I found Goofy hiding in the closet shaking.

Opening the kitchen door Goofy escaped to the freedom of the backyard.

Barry told me when we first started hanging out how he found Goofy wandering the streets of downtown Los Angeles. "I opened the door of the VW and in he jumped. Been pals ever since."

I looked down at his decaying body and whispered two words.

On the day of his funeral I learned that Barry was last seen by his sister Marilyn on the afternoon of the 25th.

Somewhere in the hours of the 25th and 26th Barry found his end.

Barry is responsible for the title of this piece. He wrote it on a 5x7" card with a one-dollar Eugene O'Neill postage stamp dead center. Barry framed his handiwork and gave it to Nancy and me for a 1977 Christmas present.

Time was running down the road for Barry Brown.

A good soul.

A haunted soul.

ROUTE 6IXTY-6IX

behind the wheel clear road ahead

puttin' this here dirty hot town behind me before another day dies.

to the windshield comes the morning light

sharp shadows, the road dust stirs, the tires rush the baking blacktop.

fly, livin' the spirit of the open road.

across the border a wandering path that leads to the deep blue of early night.

a light punch on the gas & i'm into fresh community

clean & sweet in the air, bright colors dance on white ropey lines

now is the time in the heartland of waving golden fields.

as i roll easy across shiny rails & splintered ties the shadows lengthen

then comes dark & the full moon glow.

feelin' so good on this free wheelin' drive

within the wild wind of nightfall that i throw

back my head & give out a mighty howl

howlin' just like the wolves under the midnight moonlight.

then comes dark & the full moon glow.

the road lines wind past a flow of broken shadowed dreams

past battered beaten structures, American ruins

CLOSED

High tailin' fast & away from the CLOSED to crossing the

GreatWesternPlains chasing after the moon. Solitary wandering

in search of that embracing rim of a new day where long lost

vagabonds roam the desolate landscape to yet another direction

of escape. As the golden light surrenders to a billion stars the road

lines flash towards the burned horizon. Man O, man time's flip trippin'
capturing the full framework of nature's majestic beauty. A score of
sights & sounds composed on the primeval stage where the moon shines
ghostly through the naked branches. Further, further into the night swept
away to where the dead stars race through space. Their brilliant brightness
fading O so fast in the deep blue of restless flight.

EN ROUTE

—There was a time once down yonder in those
long ago use t'bes where I wandered the 5 & 10 splintered aisles of that
corner store. Picking up a comic or a Lone Ranger 6-shooter gun, betting
my lot I'd always be flowing on the young. Now on a shadowy flash of faded
time, reckon I've seen my better days, as I'm drawn to the quiet hidden
darkness on a silent dealt breath. Lost to the solitude as I try to understand
                                        yesterday in the shape of today.

       no more fearing the disquiet within the haunt
       of life as i fully enjoy the forward of GO
       beyond the scarecrow waving fields.
       movin' onward free from want, across the border
       to the early evening blue, that is choked by dark
       battling grey, which brings a drench of washing rain
       on a deserted ½ breath i steer towards a crop
       of seeded memories that are rooted upon the
       sprawling bare earth in the deep shelter of northern light.
       in the rearview dusty disappearing dreams of the long ago.

—On a weathered billboard

JUST WHEN YOU THINK
YOU HAVE LIFE FIGURED OUT
ADIOS

—An almighty golden-streaked wind blows the dusty

long ago to the desolation of a desert night a distant train whistle awakens
moon-shadowed vagabonds that roam the vanishing landscape against a misty
red-blue horizon. Solitary wandering on the long & winding that leads
                                towards the majesty of nature.

      —A whisper, You felt no fear when the journey began.
            Have no fear when the journey ends.

        swept away
        riding upon the wild fresh wind of
                spirited flight

WHY, ARIZONA

"Hi, it's me. Uh, southwest Arizona, Route 85. No, I'm not kiddin'. Don't know exactly. There's a road sign ahead...can't make it out. Getting dark. Beautiful red horizon. I'm standing in what must be the last phone booth. At least one of the last. You don't see many phone booths these days. Changes, yeah. You got my note didn't you? Yeah, I know it didn't say anything about Arizona. What things? Didn't take anything with me. Didn't think I'd be gone for more than an hour. Picked up a few things along the way. Just wanted to take a drive is all. Yeah, yeah, I know it's been a week. Went by fast, huh? Well, it did for me. Sorry you worried. Called later that day. Got my message, didn't you? Then you know. Left you a number of messages, but every time I called you were out. Yeah, yeah, I know you have a life. I'm fine...doin' fine. Seen a lot of the country. Nice to be driving free. Goin' where you want. Changing skies. Wonderful feeling. No, no, I don't mean to imply anything. Nothing. Don't know, woke out of this dark driving rain of a nightmare. Disturbing. You were sleeping so peaceful. Got up and made coffee. After two cups I got it into my head to take a drive. Was around three-thirty. Heard the train whistle down in Sawmill. Was a beautiful early morning for countin' stars. Thought I'd be back before you woke, or at least by sunrise. But then at first light found myself crossin' the borderline to farms of Virginia. Go figure. What? No, I wasn't going to...didn't even think of heading there. No, was just driving. Just driving, is all. Folks were late afternoon porch rockin' in Sweetwater, Tennessee. Was by this lake in Georgia. Canoe fishing. Layers of pink-blue clouds. Across the way the church bells playin' ROCK OF AGES. In Alabama hundreds of seagulls on a freshly plowed field. Did some rockin' myself in Magnolia, Mississippi. An old man with dark spirited eyes was

49

rockin' on a store porch next to his dog. He told me of his wife wanting to see faraway places, but never had the money. When she passed away he gave her ashes to the wind. Said, 'The wind is like a dream, takes you many places. Now God Bless, my lovely best friend is seein' it all.' Then he softly sang this wayfarin' gospel. Henry would've loved the thought of wind like a dream, don't ya think? You bet, yeah. Wind like a dream. I fell asleep rockin'. When I woke they were gone. Early Wednesday morning I cross the Mississippi River. Was about 30 miles north of Baton Rouge when I came across this roadside café in Morganza. Turns out it was the café used in EASY RIDER. Remember the rednecks word bashin' Fonda, Hopper and Nicholson? Yeah, well, now the owner has a photo from RIDER on the wall along with a group shot of the rednecks with Fonda. Hopper and Nicholson. Fonda's flashin' a peace sign. Funny strange. From Louisiana I drove southwest into Texas. Passed through Dime Box, Dripping Springs and Luckenbach. Yeah, right, the Luckenbach that Willie Nelson sings about. A long stretch of Texas, then it was into New Mexico on Route 10. Saw a sign for Juarez. Temptin' thoughts of crossin' but didn't wanna deal with any Mexican authorities. Steady flow of blacktop through Las Cruces. Passed through Silver City and Mulecreek on 180. Route 78 brought me into Arizona. Route 666 south got me back onto 10. No, not Route 66. Was 666...I'm sure, yeah. Route 66 doesn't even exist anymore, taken over by 40. I mean 66 still exists in the memory of old-timers. Guess that includes you and me, eh? Okay, okay...yeah, yeah, you're not an old-timer. Sorry. Yeah, well, anyway 66 was in northern Arizona. Wrote all the routes and towns down if you're wondering. Well, just in case you were. Reading all this off that note pad you gave me. You know, the leather bound one. Had it in the glove compartment. Finally getting some use out of it. Yeah, at long last. After Tucson caught 86 south which brought me onto the Papago Indian Reservation. That was really something. You would've loved it. Got you a turquoise... What? Say again? What are you...talking? Are you serious? No, this has nothing to do with Joan Didion's book PLAY IT AS IT LAYS, or the movie with Tuesday Weld. When's the last time I brought that up? Yeah, well, this has nothing to do with Weld's character Maria drivin' the Los Angeles freeway and Pacific Coast Highway. You're stretching this way outta...with all due respect, you are. Went for a drive a few days back. Okay, yeah, a week ago. And out of this drive you think I'm trying to be like some character in a book? Don't you think that's a little strange? Yes, I accept that I'm strange, but I sure wasn't thinking of...yeah, yeah, I know I talked about it a lot. But that was years ago. Took a drive. No more to it. Never intended for it to stretch into a week. Never did. Something just took hold of me is all. That's the plain and simple of it. I'm sorry you're upset. Really am. You know, if anything, this has somewhat to do with EASY RIDER. Remember the campfire scene when Nichols said something about how this used to be a helluva good country, you know, in response to the bigoted words of the rednecks? Yeah, well, as I was driving I thought to myself, when was it a helluva good country? Indians massacred. Slavery. Civil War. Great Depression. McCarthy's Red Scare. The Kennedy's, Malcolm X and Dr. King assassinated. Students killed by the National Guard at Kent State. Homeless Vets. Students killing students. It's nuts. Gettin' crazier. Yeah, I know. Good does outweigh. America's beautiful freedom. Just gets directed in craziness from time to time. Yeah, you're so right. Power it is. And it's never gonna change. Thought after Nixon resigned it might. You know, a few lessons learned. Man, what was I thinking? Naïve me. Imagine if lessons were learned. Just imagine. Yeah, yeah, guess this is the most I've talked in a long time. Should hit the road more, eh? Listen, I want you to know that I appreciate you. Always have. Always will be appreciatin'. You've always been there. Has been a passage of time, yeah. Such a passage. So different back then, in the long ago used to be's. Yeah, yeah, everything a long time ago. Everything. Right, old-timers we are, yeah. Don't have to apologize. One thing for sure we were never second-hand hearts. I know you do. How very much you do. Me too. A day doesn't go by without missing Henry. Ours to remember. It always will be. I'm gonna head to Arlington. Be the wind. Like a dream, yeah. I will, yes. You know I will. You're my blessing. Always."

The burning horizon silhouettes the man in the old phone booth. After a loving goodbye, he pauses, then slowly hangs the phone. Pushing himself from the booth he gets behind the wheel, turns the headlights on, and drives west. Forty yards up the blacktop he brakes to a stop and stares out the windshield at the road sign which is framed by the darkening red. After a long silence he looks to the rearview mirror, he then makes a slow U-turn, but no sooner is he headed east, then he yanks the wheel into another U-turn. And another. And another. With each U-turn the headlights sweep the road sign.

DESTINATION LOUISIANA BLUES

Tucked behind the wheel

dark early mornin' drive

headlights spear a straight path

for the rustin' wheels

i am the only one on the road

on the dark early morn

no one else in this vanishin' landscape,

but then hatched from the

haunting darkness

man O, man

a MoNsTeR truck rumbly ROARS

"Must be chasin' in on 90" I whisper to the night

me, I drive smooth&easy in the dark early,

Michael Parks sneaks out of the radio

singin' about all those folks meetin' up on Basin Street,

saxie&sexy they be dancin' in the street,

then soothin' lyrics paint a vivid picture

of the breezes off the wheel

the muddy Mississippi,

i drive on easy&smooth drummin'

yeh, I follow the road signs south,

so many miles to cover

but soon I will be meetin' up

  with that Life on Basin Street,

& then I will be caught up in

the sultry & dangerous vibe of Bourbon Street
where jazz notes echo
in shadowy haunts
  yeh, I drive south into them dyin' miles
to that paradise New Orleans
bathed in blue note dreams
"Go saxman, go"
they are dancin'
in the Vieux Carre,
yeh, I drive into that vision
that I dream around the bend
down Louisiana way.

WINTER DARKNESS

As the winter light fades to darkness the candle light shadows her face,

-Was a beautiful snow today.

-Surely was.

-Another day goodbye. Passing fast.

-Yep.

-Doesn't your mother live close by?

-Here in town.

-For whatever reason I thought as much. Does taking care
of me take much time away from her?

-No.

-I wouldn't want that. I mean being the one that causes her
missing the snowfall with you.

-All's good

-Ah, the haunting cross of homespun time.

-What?

-Wrinkled bark m'think. These days of winter. Was when I was a small
girl, a pond across the road. In the winter the bare white
limbs. The icy coated pond layered with frozen leaves. Snow

storming drifting across the road. Truly a wonderland. No
wrinkled bark in sight. Appreciating every breath.

                                            -You feeling all right?

-Oh, yeah, just saying is all. Think I'm going to turn in.

                                        -Have yourself a good sleep.

-Hopefully this old head of mine will stir-up some pretty snowfall
dreams. Good night.

-After kissing her forehead he blows out the flame,
then softly
whispers,

                                                    -Night mom.

WRINKLES

She told me I was getting old
I didn't feel any difference in myself
I carried on pretty much day after day

She told me I was getting old,
didn't have the time for her that I used to,
times passes for everyone
(no shit)
She shouldn't be surprised
I went out for a walk
when I came back she had her bags packed
She looked at me
I looked at her
"I'm going" she said
Me,
I turned around went out the door.
When I hit the corner I stood still,
but then after a few seconds I took a step
& smiled.
(As I got off the train 2 days later
in New Orleans I was still thinking about her.
I did love her. But, she wanted it all her way.
Only her way. I went to the French Quarter.
A few hrs. later I felt very much better.
Very much so. Or so you would have guessed.)

VOWS

-Slowly we moved through the silence
of the desolate snowdrift, past the naked
limbs, seeking refuge from the bare bone wind.

As daylight faded to a half-moon of guiding light,
we were shone a path to a deserted church,
where we lay upon a cold splintered pew.
Fingers entwined, hugging for warmth,
we exchanged vows of love. Then prayed
through the night for the shine of tomorrow.

BREATH

The horizon rushes up to meet the ribbon of road that snakes west. Been fast and loose going on many days. No rhyme or reason to my yellow road line direction. Flowing on the go. Traveling forward resisting the urge to take that backward glance that may awaken the yesterdays hidden within the darkness. Yeah, no way to escape those back-traveling roads. Then like the cat curiosity lures. I raise my eyes to the rearview and there the emotions are strung up waving in the wind. Around a flashing turn I'm captured by a mapped spidery direction of time.

I roll out of the deep darkness of an autumn grave where the stripes of America wave, and into the rolling thunder of heavy duty rock & roll that fills the interior of the forest green '68. Mustang. "Yeah, let it be. Roll me into that the touchstone of all shook up." And there I am crowded between sweaty beating bodies where the bass and drums are cookin'. The first three notes and the crowd goes wild screaming out the lyrics. Strong players with their invisible string guitars. Strong players drumming their body parts. Yeah, the human drive of it. Picks you up and drives home that joy. Not the same old thing time after time. Might sound like that to some, but not to this here body. It's like leaning over a pinball machine, watching that shiny ball scramble between those colored lights, yeah, that is rock & roll to me. Not knowing where that killer beat is headed. And you're coiled so tight in the burning rain of one false move that could push you towards a coffin of silence. But screw it, burn out young, least you don't have to spend no time lined up in venetian blind hallways where staring eyes are hidden within quiet shadows.

An old man with long white hair comes around the corner with canvas, brush and rainbow palette. His hand aged with the pain of suffering touches the brush in the wet paint. The brush strokes a grand sweep across the canvas. A gold shade tinged with a trace of green. Once again, the brush touches gently on the palette's colors. A gentle stroke and the gold green is host to a brilliant sun-filled encompassing blue. Breathing softly his hand works delicately soothing his colored life into perspective. The old man touches the thin brush into the yellow brown wetness. The stroke caresses the canvas in a breeze of golden grass. Staring eyes no longer hidden are alive with a colorful glow of deep quiet dreaming.

I keep the Mustang on smooth drive as the rearview closes down. A long stretch of winding yellow lures me to a roofed comforting rain where the alluring figure of Paris kisses me softly, "Je t'adore." "I thought I lost you." "Forever always we break day together." And off we go to a corner of landscape where Paris entwines me in a simmering flow of passionate heat under full limbed trees and haunting L-shaped rooms that are baked behind shaded high noon windows. A dance of raw emotions. Paris smiles, "L'amour en fuite." Then to my clouded eyes, "Love on the run." I had to reason that I was dreaming as I found myself deep within the bare naked limbs. Embracing our solitude Paris and I go nice and easy to the scorched hungry hours where we're captured by the dancing moods of rainy light. Through the breath brushed down the lonely moon. Paris traces the moon's face on the moist pane, "The room is crying." In the scrambled distance a child-like voice, "Smile lonely moon, smile."

I stir to four walls of comforting rain. "Am I waking from a dream within a dream of deep rainy sleep?" In her white drenched nightgown Paris whispers, "Midnight hours. Asleep." My eyes trace the waltzing shadows that climb the walls. In the faraway corner Paris is dancing in small tight moves around an old rocking chair, "Je vous aime beaucoup." A bold brush of wet invites a gentle stroke which arouses the intoxicating curves that form Paris by moonlight. "J'y suis, j'y reste." A soft red-sky kiss, "Here I am, here I stay."

60

On weathered porch steps a hand-carved music box plays Always, as a girl and boy child wave the stripes of America, "Freedom in Paradise." A deep kiss closes the darkness. "See me in the moon's white glow, I'll sing you a lullaby." Breath deepens.

By the burnt red-clouded streaks of morning light the Mustang peacefully roams Chief Joseph Pass in Southwest. Montana. The wandering road ropes me into a valley of rolling thunder clouds. A dozen miles up the asphalt in the vicinity of Wise River, I settle over a black coffee in the One Horse Town Café just as driving rain attacks the small-boxed windows. Staring out at the whirlwind my head stumbles back to the autumn of America waving. A circle of comings and goings in a passage of loaded time. A scattered direction of back porch memories. For better or worse there's no escape. A brilliant lightning flash awakens the dark sky. I count, "One Mississippi, two-Mississippi," then comes a mighty thunderclap which awakens in my head a crop of words from Jim Harrison's novel Farmer, "On very rare occasions life will offer up something as full and wonderful as anything the imagination can muster." I raise my slow dance of steam black to Paris by moonlight, "To the very rare."

A mighty curve of northeast miles leads me to a raised thumb on a lonely stretch of road in Fargo, North Dakota. A dark-haired beauty wearing faded jeans and fatigue jacket eyes my weathered head through the passenger window. I nod howdy and rise my fingers in peace.

After going a good country mile, I say to the thumb-tripper, "It's been a most peculiar year." Out of the corner of my eye I see her dark features turn to me, "I hear that. Strange days."

"Yeah," I nod to the roadway, then take a sidelong framing of dark hair, "I like your Dream Catchers."

In reflex she caresses the sky-blue turquoise stones captured on the silver feathers of the earrings.

"Thanks."

"You bet."

"A present from the long ago."

"The long ago I know. Here sits a backwards traveler."

"Yeah?"

"Yep."

As the miles mount in silence I'm in the rearview of a deep quiet rainy night where I'm scrawling dreamy on a lonely moon.

"You okay?"

In the flash of a road line I'm on the firing line of the here and now, "Yeah, just lost to the long ago is all."

"Good?"

"Eh?"

"Your long ago."

Under a deep ripe breath, "Heavy duty."

"Sounds inviting."

"Rare occasions."

"That sure says something."

After a silent sweep of blacktop, "There was a time once..."

On the outskirts of Blue Earth, Minnesota, I whisper, "Howdy," to the early morning moon as dark-hair sings an old-fashioned tune about wayfarin' strangers.

An hour of miles up the road as we pass through Spirit Lake, Iowa, I soft voice to the pink-red horizon, "Daybreak."

Sunk deep in the passenger seat dark-hair yawns, "Fresh...today."

Shadows slowly gather on the landscape.

72ND & CENTRAL PARK WEST

Rats have been
discovered
among
The Peace Trees
among
The Peace Plants
in
Strawberry Fields
Imagine.

APPROACH

The man enters the park and slowly walks the winding paths. With every step he appreciates fully the surround of beauty. As the man comes to a clearing he stops, smiles, then walks forward.

"Would you care for a coffee?"

The woman looks to the man, "Excuse me?"

"A coffee. I'm going to get a container of coffee. They have very good coffee at that deli across the park. Very good containers. Keeps the coffee hot. Would you like a container of coffee?"

"No...no thank you."

The man stands in silence. He looks around the park, then turns back to the woman, "Why is it men approach women, but not the other way around? I would love for a woman to approach me. Ask if I'd like a coffee. Women never do. We, the man, always have to approach. Why can't the woman approach?"

"You're asking me?"

"I see you," he smiles.

"Pardon?"

"I see you."

"I don't follow what you're..."

"You see me."

"I see you...yes."

"But I have to approach."

"Approach?"

"Yes."

"I guess."

"You're beautiful. I mean that in the best way possible. No offense."

"Thanks," she smiles. "I guess."

"See."

"What?"

"You wouldn't have said that to me."

"What, beautiful?"

"No... anything." He sits on the edge of the bench. "You wouldn't have said anything. We wouldn't be talking now if...well, if it wasn't for me approaching you."

"No... I guess not."

"Don't you think that's a shame? After all there's so little time."

"How do you mean?"

"Haven't you noticed how fast time is passing?"

"No."

"You haven't?"

"No."

"I have," he says. "It's passing. Passing very fast. Perhaps it's my state of mind. Here it is Monday..."

"No, it's Friday."

"What's what I was about to say. Here it is Monday..."

"No, it's Friday."

"Yes, I know."

"But you keep saying Monday."

"What I mean to say is...here it is Friday..."

"Yes."

"Back there...a few days back...Monday."

"Yes."

"Now here is what I was originally saying. Here it is Monday," he holds up his hand, "Whoa, don't say anything. And the next thing you know it's Friday. The days they pass so fast."

"Yes...I guess. Yes, I've found that to be true."

He leans back on the bench, "You've got great legs."

"Pardon?"

"Great eyes."

"My eyes..."

"Great hair. You've got it all."

"Thank you," she smiles."

"But you wouldn't have said that to me."

"Well..."

"You wouldn't have. We have to approach. We...the man has to say those things. Women get offended if a man walks up to them on the street and... well, says those things."

"Well I..."

"But if a woman would walk up to me on the street and say those nice things I wouldn't be offended. I would be pleased. It would make me happy. Happy that someone thought nice things about me. Would make my day. Did it make you happy when I said what I did?"

"Well it's nice to hear nice things..." her voice fades.

"So why is it a woman can't approach a man and say the same things. That's equality. Why can't we all just get to the point and stop the games."

"Games?"

"Well, isn't that what it is? The games between men and women."

"I don't know."

"Well call it what you will. All I know is that we always have to approach. Did you ever approach?"

"No," she smiles shyly.

"Did you ever want to...ever want?"

"Yes..."

"But you didn't."

"No."

"Why not?"

"Oh, I don't know...perhaps it would've given..."

"What?"

"Well, the wrong signals."

"Those being."

"You know...what men expect." Then she adds, "Want."

"To be friends?"

"No." She shakes her head smiling, "To have..."

"Dinner?"

"Well, sometimes...yes...but..."

"What?"

"Well, the dinner that leads to..."

"A walk."

"A walk?"

"Yes...home."

"Well, yes."

"In the rain."

"The rain?"

"Yes," he nods. "I love to walk in the rain. A light rain."

"So do I."

"There's something about walking in a light rain on a warm evening. Something very comfortable about the rain. A light rain."

"Yes," she smiles.

"Even when I'm home. In my apartment. I watch the rain on the window. How it tears down the window. I watch the lights reflect on the wet street."

"Yes."

"There's a liquor store across from where I live. The window is filled with colorful neon signs. The Reds. Greens. Blues. Yellows. The magic of those colors on the rainy street."

"Yes...very nice," she adds in a near whisper.

"It is. Very nice. Comforting. I don't know why. But it is. For some reason...it makes me feel...safe. Safe in the world. Warm in the world. And I watch the colorful lights."

They sit in silence.

"There are lights across from where I live," she says. "A Chinese restaurant. Very colorful lights. I watch the lights reflect on the street. I listen to Mozart or Beethoven and watch the brilliant colors on the wet street."

"Peaceful."

"Very."

"It's nice to have the still every once in a while."

"Yes."

"The world is so restless."

"So on edge."

"Yes."

"People scared of one another."

"Yes."

"But to be able to have that moment...those moments of stillness."

"Yes," he says softly.

"Winter nights. Looking out the window. Snow passing before the street lamp. The easy snow fall. Covering over the dirt. Making it all clean and good. One moment. Or two. Clean and good. To look out late at night and see that happen. All outside my window. Comforting in a still life. To be lost in those late hours of night. In a clean white silence of peace. Lost within myself and the whiteness."

"To be still."

"Framed within the stillness."

"Yes."

"Listening to Mozart."

"Yes."

"Beethoven."

"Yes."

"You agree?"

"Yes."

"You agree a lot."

"Yes," he smiles.

"Do you ever disagree?"

"Yes."

"Do you disagree...a lot?"

"No," he shakes his head.

"No?"

"Life is too short for fussing and fighting."

"It is...yes."

"Too short. I mean here it is Friday."

"And it was just Monday."

"Yes," he nods.

"Went by fast."

"Very."

"Yes."

"Who would want to fill that with fussing..."

"And fighting," she quickly adds.

"Exactly."

"Not me."

"Or me." The man looks across the park then turns to the woman. "Would you care for a coffee?"

"Excuse me?"

"I was coming in for my second approach," he smiles.

"Oh."

"Would you care for a coffee?"

"No. No thank you...no."

The man looks across the park in silence. The smile fades from his face.

"How about tea?" She smiles.

"Tea?"

"Yes."

"Absolutely."

"Milk. One sugar."

"One sugar. Milk."

"Yes," she smiles.

"I'll be right back."

"Okay."

"Here I go."

"Wait." She reaches out and touches his arm.

"What?"

"Your eyes."

"My eyes?"

"You have pretty eyes," she smiles.

"Pretty?"

"Very expressive."

"Expressive..."

"Yes."

"Thanks...thank you," he smiles.

"You have a nice smile."

"Thank you."

"Would it be all right if we forget the coffee. Forget the tea."

"Forget?"

"Yes."

"You said yes...yes to the tea."

"I still say yes."

"I don't understand."

"Come back to my place," she says softly.

"Your..."

"Yes...my place. I'll make you coffee. Hot coffee in a nice cup. We can listen to Beethoven and..."

"Mozart."

Their eyes are on one another.

"I'm Sarah."

"I'm Henry."

They extend their hands to shake. Then they don't so much as shake, but just hold each other's hand.

"It looks like rain," Sarah smiles.

"Rain would be nice."

"Yes."

"Yes," Henry smiles.

Hands locked they are lost to the shadows of the surround of beauty.

GO, GONE

it's been a most peculiar year, indeed a strange year at that

too late by a summer grave the coffin into view

I held the stripes of America, plus a rose game me too

shadows crawled the walls on the returning rainy nights

lonely, so afraid

the horror it was to fight

—3 days down the line into the following week found faith
on a roadside Kansas City billboard. Climbed aboard. Been
moving forward on a rootless freedom getaway of crossing
borders ever since. Time flip tripping me so as to capture
every sight and sound.

Feeling fine as I drift along past shady trees on a flow of
fresh wind.

By the burnt red morning light, I ride the wandering
crooked road into a valley of dark rolling thunder clouds. A
dozen miles up the blacktop I settle over black coffee just
as a heavy-duty drench attacks the small-boxed windows.

staring out at the whirlwind I'm taking into a reflection of
snatched time.

                an explosion howls as a beat so fierce,
                shape shifting smoke lingers, settles,
                traveling eastward with the earth on a darkling
                plain between white hot images of truth & fiction
                        where bones lay alone among the shadows.

    A mighty thunderclap awakens the long ago Walden
words of Thoreau: I come to the solitude, where the
problem of existence is simplified.

    Going right yonder down that stretched out open road
where the golden plains rollout vast as the sea.

                a hinterland

                odyssey

    The sun breaks through yawning clouds as I pass a
weathered hand-carved cross that marks a highway death.

                a daybreak

                whisper, Vaya con Dios.

    Prowling onward towards an authentic life after dealing
with the crowded beaten path. A rearview glance takes me

back to that passage of strange time within a most peculiar

year, then

ever so slowly a muddy swirl creeps

upon that dark yesteryear grave of sunken

time, where we pushed the last hours before

the closing breath, shadows were crawling

the walls when the rain came

afraid so lonely,

we struggled from under the buried blanket

of deep darkness as the day before shallow

flow rose under the naked winter limbs.

after the deluge

off into the divine presence of something

that cannot be seen, a journey through

white-drenched rhythms that stretch past

a comfortable path onto a rebirth of beauty,

so unlike anywhere

I've ever been.

go,

gone

PIANO, TEXAS

Sitting over a cup of black coffee at a small roadside diner outside Piano, Texas, I scribble on a napkin a few of the lyrics from Willie Nelson's *Remember the Good Times*, "Don't spend a moment unhappy, invaluable moments gone with the leakage of time, as we leave on our separate journeys, moving west to the sun, to a place buried deep in our minds."

So many unhappy in this here day and age. Who can blame them. Just last week in Nickel Mines, Pennsylvania, 5 Amish girls were killed in a tragic shooting. And around the world the maiming and killing of the innocent. I try and make the best out of each day that I'm dealt so I can stay on the far other side of unhappy. Sometimes it's as simple as parking my pickup late in the day and watching the horizon eat up the burning red. I move slow around the landscape, picking up odd jobs, then move on. There was a time when I was tied to one roof, but then came September 11th. One week later I made my escape into the unknown of day to day living. I'd often thought about doing it in my younger days, but I always came up with an excuse for putting it off. You know, protecting the back. Playing it safe. Doing the comfortable. But truth be told nothing has been more comfortable than rolling around America. Seeing the new and different each day. Getting fully into the rhythm of life.

A few years before my escape my lady friend Molly came at me outta the blue. Talk about protecting the back. Man, she saw where I was at before I even clutched and got myself into gear.

"You're a throwback to another time," she said. "The way you go through life. This starving artist thing you do. Depriving yourself of..."

"I don't deprive myself."

"You don't want anything. How can you not want anything? Need anything? All you have is that pickup truck, books and music. Nothing else. You're like this vagabond. This wild seed drifting down the road. And your talk of Thoreau and Van Gogh. Henry Miller. Bukowski. Route 66. Smith and Hickock."

"Who?"

"Capote's *In Cold Blood*. Dick and Perry, you know?"

"Man, you're all over the map," I smiled.

"Yeah, man," she threw at me, "just like you've been. And we sure can't forget Kerouac. I remember all of it. Remember well. It's all I ever heard day into night. Year after year. All your driftin' drifters."

"Where did this drifting stuff come from? Looking at me like I'm some kind of hobo. I wanted nothing but the best for you. Did my best to take care of you." I threw up my hands in surrender, then after a long pause. "The people have plenty..."

"What?"

"They have plenty and they want more, but in the end, they have nothing."

"Where did you get that?"

"I see folks scrambling for their share of possessions. But for the most part, these very same folks are miserable. And it's amazing, sometimes the richest ones are the most miserable. They're so caught up in the pursuit of things, that they've lost sight of the real pursuit."

"Which is?"

"Happiness. I may not have much, but I see happiness. Enjoy life. The living of it. I don't need the framework of things to make me happy."

"Thoreau, huh?"

"Yeah, simplify, not a bad way to go."

"Like I said you're this throwback to another time."

"I would like nothing better than to wash this all away. To say the right words before you're snatched away."

She choked up a hard-bitten laugh, "Snatched?"

"Yeah...away."

"I'm not being snatched away. You pushed me away."

"No, I..."

"It was your way or no way. Trips. Restaurants. Movies you wanted to see."

"You know that's not true."

"You think I wanted to see Bergman movies? Read subtitles? I wanted entertainment. Some laughs. Not angst. How many times did we see Persona and Scenes from a Marriage? And the ones with your girlfriend..."

"What are you talking?"

"Those French films. Particularly that one where she played a prostitute..."

"Anna Karina. Godard's My Life to Live. Beauty."

"Yeah, I'd have to hear how beautiful and sexy your Anna was. You even wrote that story with a dream sequence. Seductive black-and-white images of Anna unreeling, right?"

"Yeah, on a brick dead-end alley wall."

"And Anna smiling, 'Art and beauty are life.'"

"You've got one helluva memory."

"No, it was just that you were so caught up in this bohemian life style and I was dragged along."

"Dragged?"

"Yes, dragged."

A long silence of lost puzzling years fill my head.

"Hate to think that I dragged a body down..."

"Needin' a hot cup are ya?"

I look up at a snow-white haired waitress holding a pot of coffee. "No, thanks."

"I thought ya called me over."

"No, guess I was just thinking out loud."

"Yeh, I catch myself doin' that now and again. Writin' a novel are ya?"

"No, just doing a bit of scribbling."

"That sure is a load of napkin writin'. Surely is."

"Just get carried away from time to time."

"Hear that I do."

In the following quiet she deals me the most beautiful early morning smile. The kind of smile that graced me way back when. Looking to escape my lost long ago used to be's I motion over to the corner booth where a cat is roaming. "That's a might big cat."

"Oh, that just be Audie patrolin' the tiles huntin' down the mice before they can get to your plate."

"Audie as in Murphy?"

"Yeah, you're in his home state, ya know? Just think the most decorated soldier of World War II born and raised just north of here in Hunt County. That's like 50 miles south of the Red River. Some years after Audie was awarded the Congressional Medal of Honor my young self read in the newspaper that Audie said, "In solitude my dreams make sense. Nobody to dispute or destroy them."

"Dreams make sense."

"Yep."

"Sounds good."

"Audie strung together a nice flow of words awright. Was truly terrible when he died like he did, y'know in that plane crash in 1971. All that Audie went through in the war and then to die like that."

"You really know your stuff."

"You betcha. At least when it comes to Audie. Like you just now said, y'know about getting carried away. Audie's my carried away. Our hero. Yes indeed. How 'bout me freshen that cup of yours?"

'No thanks. Appreciate. I'm outta here."

"Where ya headed?"

"Don't know, just goin'."

"I'd like to be on an unknown like that. Endless possibilities. Looks t'be a grand day to be out under, but then again ain't each and every day grand."

"You bet."

I finish off my coffee, spread a few extra coins on the counter, then swivel on the stool to the screen door exit, but before I can push myself from the red plastic seat, I'm back to the counter scribbling Thoreau, "Contact – rocks, trees, wind on our cheeks, the solid earth, the actual world. Contact, contact. Who are we? Where are we going?"

Sharp morning shadows. Road dust stirs. Tires ruch the blacktop. Road lines flow past weathered and battered structures. American ruins CLOSED. Shadows lengthen. Red blaze dies to the horizon. Coyotes howl at the ghostly haunt of the moon. Dream under a billion stars. Pink-blue early morning clouds. Yellow-lined blacktop. A faraway voice, "Ain't each and every day grand." I look to the rearview. "You betcha."

HOMELESS

Are the
homeless
registered to vote,
Their tents were
torn down the
other night (5July89)
in Tompkins Park
by New York's finest,
A thousand
lower east side
citizens
raised voices
in protest,
The rains came hard
that night
The streets
were flooded,
Are the homeless
registered to vote,
Watch out
Mayor Koch.

DETOURS

i hold the Bic pen to the hot bulb of naked light-been checkin' the level of ink on the daily-would've thought after all i've written the ink would've gone down a bit-but I have yet to see any sign-faster & harder with the Bic-layin' down letters-fightin' 'em into words-battlin' the ink hard & fast by the naked bulb of light

-Everything works out the way it's supposed to. We had our time. Lost it.

-We still have time.

-Time of what?

-A time once upon a time...to believe we were innocent once upon a time. Running free. Hopes. Dreams. Do you recall, sitting across from one another for many years?

-What do you mean?

-It's what your father said shortly before we married. Said, "Be sure it's the real thing, because you'll be sitting across the table from one another for many years."

-Believe he said years and years.

-Yeah, right. Years and...

-Years.

-Right, yeah. "Devastating blow to our antiquated systems."

-What?

-Just remembering back years and years ago when we saw "Easy Rider." Remember how you liked Nicholson's Venutian space talk. I was more taken with the bikes. Fonda and Hopper riding the southwest. Beauty of Monument

Valley. Across the border to Louisiana to Mardi Gras high times. Final campfire, Fonda, "We blew it." Outside walking in November silence i said...

-That you loved me. Caught me by surprise. Didn't know what to say.

-For whatever reason had to say it then and there. I remember how good...very good it was between us. There's something to be salvaged here.

-Salvaged?

-You know what I mean.

-We blew it.

-You can't forget the memories. The good times.

-They're not forgotten. This now is the time. This is what we've become.

-I'm sorry.

-Sorry?

-I am. I'm sorry for taking it all for granted.

-There was a time once when we made time for each other. A time when we enjoyed the stillness together.

-We still have plenty of good times ahead. I know we do. It's not too late. We still...still have time.

-Time...

Man O, man the time is flashin' as i'm warehouse stackin' the sheets of white- that someone, someday might come to read-but if they don't that's OK-bottom line i write 1st for me

-This photo of Lucinda reminds me of Bergman's "Persona" poster with Liv Ullmann. Clean sharp light. Blonde hair. Full lips. Penetrating eyes.

-Man, those eyes...

-Whoa, that sounds mighty...

-Yeah, had herself such---penetrating eyes. Unfortunately, didn't have true appreciation back then. Yeah, way too much taken for granted in that long ago.

-What's with you?

-This here yearbook is what. Goin' back. Yeah, goin' way back in time. Rememberin' Duke. Man, I really believed after that horror...would never be another. No lessons learned. The head honchos promisin' everythin' between here and there. Best to just move ahead doin' the appreciatin'. Look here at Duke framed so strong and confident. And this football shot.

-Duke could really scoot 'n' boot. Remember his '52 Ford?

-Yeah, the green monster rollin' Penn Street.

-When Penn Street was worth rolling.

-Man, it used to be a helluva city. From colorful neon lights, majestic movie houses and crowded sidewalks to silent emptiness.

-So much for progress.

-Time a-fallin'.

-That's it. Falling away.

-Duke's last line in his last letter stateside, "I'm running out of time." Killed a month later.

-Nam had no mercy. Haunting days into nights.

-Took to the hide after Duke's death. Although Lucinda said I was always on the hide. No, elusive is what she said. And I guess elusive prêt-near sums up our relationship. Good friends passin' through the 60s. Our truest...clearest time was a few weeks before I was headin' into the Army. Met by chance on Penn Street. At least two years since we laid eyes on each other. But felt like yesterday. Off on the motorcycle to midnight red wine. Time of innocence. Ridin' the days into nights before facin' the hard march. Lucinda was there the mornin' I boarded the train for Fort Dix. She was a comfortin force throughout those wearin' basic trainin' months.

-Sounds like you had a good thing going, what happened?

-Like I said didn't have true appreciation. By the time I learned some good life lessons Lucinda was outta sight. Heard she's living in Thoreau, New Mexico, off ol' Route 66. Man o, man it's been a flashin' passage of time.

-We're getting close to that park bench.

-Eh?

-Simon & Garfunkle's "Old Friends."

-Weather beaten sittin' still lives.

-Heading there brother.

-That line from Willie Nelson's song surely says it, "I wonder when the hell did I get older." Yeah, runnin' outta time. Bless you Duke.

as the Bic scrambles by the bulb's naked red hot light i'm outta the corner to fight the good fight-yeah, i'm here to tell ya the ink is gonna go down tonight

Seconds later the ink dead ends. Try fighting the alphabet into words once again but that black ink Bic wasn't obliging. As I lay the Bic atop the yellow-lined pad, "Heard it said, Nothing happens 'til it must." Rickety stairs to cracked paves. At the top of the building a full moon starry night. Around the corner at Rudy's Bar and Grill I catch sight of my reflection in the mirrored window. Moving up close I look deep into the eyes, "Gimme an answer." Blink. "That's it, huh? A few minutes later I slide behind the wheel of my yellow taxi. Drive the night. Roundup ideas for the Bic. After a handful of good fares I park by the Bowery Diner. Sitting over a steaming black coffee I stare out the soiled window at the passing parade of folks trying to do their best in this here life. The Bowery caffeine wakes a long ago late night scribble: too late by a summer grave the coffin into view he holds the stripes of America-shadows crawled the walls on the returning rainy nights-lonely, so afraid-the horror it was to fight. Blinking away that time ago I gulp the last warm drops of black, then it's back behind the wheel. Blaring horns. Subways cursing the underground. Jackhammers pounding. Neon blossoms of steel canyon corner bars. Jazz, rock 'n roll & classical strings ride the waves for all the lost wine souls & perfumed tailored ladies. Steam rises from the bowels of the city. A warm might wind blows a clear view of the Hudson. Flow river, flow.

At an intersection in the East Village a stocky man with a battered face jacks open the door to my taxi. His pudgy bruised hand grips a Smith & Wesson .38. The instant before the bluish barrel burrows hard into my temple I see myself smiling on a child's swing. Sailing way up high hoping for a good night dream.

Reaching for a brilliant glorified shine he falls from the swing into a deep dark tunnel where there comes an explosion. Red slowly snakes. Eyes are dead-set blue on the rearview. The taxi jumps the curb and drifts across a deserted lot where it comes to rest against a pile of bricks and rumble. Through the afternoon the taxi idles under the broil of August. At dusk the last drop of gas flows through the carburetor. The engine sputters, then comes the still coffin silence inside the taxi as the air conditioner gives up its last breath of cold.

PAINTED DESERT

Wolves howl as clouds unmask a ghostly moon. Buried in my sleeping bag I'm swept into a long dark tunnel of bleeding night where I'm steam pulsing at a shadowy female, "Man, there was a time once when I stick snapped that snare just like Dennis Wilson. Yeah, we were rockin' in that fast lane. Monster drive. Then came war. My buddy Duke gets blown away. Twenty-year old battler. And my pal Doc, did himself two tours as a Black Beret. Back to the World in '71, Doc wrapped his 1962 British racing green Corvette in 4th gear speed around a 1966 silver Cadillac on a haunting midnight blue of survival. On November 13th, 1982, the day the Vietnam War Memorial was being dedicated, Doc called crying. Heated memories. Doc told me a shotgun was at hand. I didn't have to be there to believe him. I knew shadings of his horror. We talked into the long night and the trigger wasn't freed. Vivre pour Vivre. Live for Life. The shadowy female looks straight through me. "You wasted all my good years." She does an about face then walks an upstream path. On my darkling plain I turn the knob of a creaky door and there I am framed in a valley of light where I'm billboarded between the unwinding images of truth and fiction. Ominous sky. Troopers scramble for shelter. "Yeah, flow a river run." "You've got spirit soldier." "Howdy Sarge." "Take shelter." Wading through the sandy mud I grab up a handful of cake and out under that storming summer wash I eat cake in the rain. Black rolling thunder clouds. Skeletons claw through a dark pooling rush of wild water. Doc holds out a helping hand as I kick at the advancing bones. A blue-eyed boy child crawls from the tangled limbs of the jungle, "Around the world is a ring of joy and peace, the problem of the ages is to find it." The American flag unfurls. Troopers march a

86

washboard trail as Duke climbs into a hand-carved coffin. The Stars and Stripes cover the blood-stained wood.

Under blue skies, yellow road lines lead me to Arizona's Painted Desert, where I'm captured by a liveliness of colors.

A hiking boot traveler wearing a bulky rucksack drifts up to my Chevy pickup, "Oxidizing of the rocks and sand, that's what created this surround of sparkling splendor."

"Beautiful."

"Blue Eyes Crying In The Rain."

"Blue eyes..."

"This song on the pickup's radio. Willie Nelson's a real troubadour."

Traveler gives a thumbs-up, then stepping over a petrified tree stump, heads southwest on the primitive landscape.

A soft rain begins to fall as Jean-Luc Godard's My Life To Live unreels on the brick wall of an alley. Seductive black-and-white images. Anna Karina smiles, "Art and beauty are life." Tramping the forest primeval I come upon words branded on a hemlock:

"I AM CONVINCED THAT TO MAINTAIN
ONE'S SELF ON EARTH IS NOT A
HARDSHIP, BUT A PASTIME,
IF WE WILL LIVE SIMPLY AND WISELY."
                              --HENRY DAVID THOREAU

"I WILL FIGHT NO MORE FOREVER."
                              --CHIEF JOSEPH

Hiking a crooked trail past the shadows of hemlocks and pines I arrive at a sun-drenched glade where hawks are soaring on the high wind. In the blue sky touching treetops John Lennon flashes a peace sign as Duke wanders the golden pastures of heaven with Audie Murphy. An aged Mexican strums a battered guitar as the shadowy female sings, "The Long and Winding Road." I think it to be a most peculiar rise and shine, but then on a full waking stretch, eyes are wide open to a clean day.

In the long shadows of late afternoon, I stop for a thumb raised in the wind. Dusty eyes catch hold of me through the half-open window, "Painted Desert, right?"

"Yep."

"What's your drive?"

"Wherever I end up."

"I'm south to Fort Apache, below Whiteriver, is that cool?"

"You got it."

After a hard ramble of rumbling miles, "I have lived through much, and now I think I have found happiness. Nature, books, music is my idea of happiness. But the only certain happiness in life is to live for others. What do you think?"

"I think, yes."

"Yeah, Tolstoy laid it down."

"Tolstoy?"

"Yes indeed. Makes me happy for that kind of thinking."

"Absolutely."

"You ever see the movie Easy rider?"

"Yeah." I smile, remembering the two-cowboy booted riders on chopped Harley's gliding through the spiritual brushed shadows of Monument Valley.

"Remember what the southern lawyer George said to Captain America and Billy about freedom, you know talking about freedom, and being free are two different things. And that when folks see a free body it scares them. I feel very fortunate to be part of freedom's landscape. You have to wonder what's going through so many of those foreign powers that they won't let their folks ride on freedom's road. Yeah, I understand that there's rough edge thinking in some corners, but I don't get why harmony's so hard."

Traveler scans the horizon, which is masked in a brilliant disguise. "Mohandis K. Gandhi and Dr. Martin Luther King, Jr. comes to mind...what with that inspirational vision."

"Vision..."

"Vision of the setting sun. Inspirational."

"Yeah, that it is. Sure is."

"I hope to be with the Great Spirits as I walk the sacred Indian land. I will pray for all to have freedom. Hopefully one day there won't be any scared folks. Imagine."

"Yeah, imagine."

As darkness closes in we cross into Fort Apache territory. Pulling off the road I park under the naked limbs of a big old tree. Stretching ourselves out of the pickup Traveler faces the good night of a billion stars, "Moon's glowing full and mighty. River flow."

"Eh?"

"U-turn of the brain. Just remembering after Billy and Captain America were shot. Bob Dylan's ballad at the end, about flowing down to the sea. Guess in this here framework, better said, river flow to the moonlight."

Traveler hoists his rucksack from the bed of the pickujp then gives the moon a sidelong glance, "Shine." Unloading a crooked smile, "Grateful for the lift."

"I'm gonna camp here, you're welcome to stay."

"Appreciate. But, I want to get on the go of the eastward turning earth. Walk Apache by night. See the wings soaring free in the shining flow."

"You've got the good spirit."

"Forward with faith into those fresh ever-changing horizons. Safe passage driver man. Peace."

"Vaya con Dios."

Ghost dancing moon shadows.

Outside Inspiration, Arizona, a thunderstorm arrives on the flip of a buffalo head. A mile up the road I pull into the sandy parking lot of the Pinto Creek Trading Post. A hand printed sign HOMEMADE FOOD fills the lower half of the window. Jumping the three steps to the weathered porch I sidewinder through the swinging doors. A brief cut of time and I'm back under the driving rain with a handful of oatmeal raisin cake. I flashback to that long ago summer storm. A circle of comings and goings in a scattered mind of directions.

I eat that fine homemade, then raise my face to the wash of the rain.

ROUTES

Zipping around the corner of 5th & Cherry he sees the streaming shape of her through the rainy windshield. Slowing to a stop he raises his fingers in peace

> -You want outta the rain?
> -That's okay, thanks.
> -Thought I saw your thumb stickin' out.
> -No, you didn't.
> -Surely did. Here take this umbrella it'll give you a touch of shelter.
> -What's that playing on the radio?
> -You like?
> -That there is the essence of cool note blowing blues.
> -Man, you really nailed that down.
> -No, those are my granny's words. Always had music playing under her roof.
> -Your granny sounds like a good-hearted woman.
> -That she was. Yeah, something was always playing. Where are you headed?
> -Don't know, just goin'.
> -Free as the breeze.
> -Somethin' like.
> -How about New Orleans?
> -Slide on in.

He drums the steering wheel as they head out of town on a one-way street on the wettest day of the year

-Keeping up with all that jazz, eh?

-You betcha.

They're the only travelers on the dark early morn. A cooling soup of a voice sneaks out of the radio singing about all those good folks meeting up on Basin Street. Jazz notes echo in the French Quarter & haunts of Bourbon Street. A whirlwind of mad burning desire bathed in rainbow neon. Down the road into paradise they go. Swing dance sinning in the Vieux Carre

-Go Saxman, go.

-Into blue note dreams.

A quiet cold grey morning sky

-This is good strong coffee.

-Know that y'can always count on a truckstop.

-Had a dream last night. Think I was in California. The sea was washing the sand white under an enormous dark blue sky.

-Never saw any white sand in California myself. Death Valley maybe.

-Then I guess it could've been anywhere. You know deep night dreaming.

-There's one thing I can tell y'bout California. South of the Monterey Peninsula is Big Sur, a mighty sight of soarin' redwoods and plungin' cliffs.

-You want?

-We're gone.

Roaring across the great American west he drums the sturdy wheel that guides the rushing tires to yet another direction of escape & the drumming never ceases.

> -What a bridge.
> -Bixby.
> -Outstanding!
> -A short span, but one helluva span.
> -Never saw a bridge that faced such an earthly vision of heaven.
> -You're in the heart of nature's wavelength.
> -The way the mountain is shrouded in fog looks like an old man, doesn't it? A big bearded old man facing the spirit of the sea.

Then & there he knew he lost the shape of her to the wilds of Big Sur. An unwinding of time south he hears her voice over the roaring Pacific blue

> -I see you tucked behind the wheel keeping a steady beat as you pass all those weathered road signs. Driving smooth.
> -Smooth drivin', yeah.
> -Down the road.
> -Yep.
> -On the go.
> -I'm smilin' on this here midnight highway.
> -Enjoying yourself.
> -I am, yeah.
> -Changing the lanes of life will do it.
> -Just appreciatin' how it spools on out.
> -It sure is good to see a body happy. I used to sit on the stoop back home and watch the folks pass by. Most of them looked so unhappy.

Their eyes were empty, didn't tell me anything. It's terrible the things
we do to each other.

-Yeah, we surely are livin' in difficult times.

-You think we were better off in the simple times that are no more?

-Put it this way y'can pretty much forget the good ol' time used t'bes.
It's crazy and gettin' crazier.

-Shame.

The starless purple sky gives way to black & blue clouds that nestle a flaming
horizon

-Into the blessed day I go.

-The road dust stirs lightly as you roll easy through a fresh
community.

-Out of the corner of my eye I'm catchin' sight of a pretty freckled-
face girl with bare feet up on the dashboard of a '55 Chevy. Yeah,
slowin' way down to check the girl-next-door-beauty. Man, there
was a time once...

-A long ago once upon a time.

-Bygone let me be.

Gas & oil. Coke bottle cold from the rusty beat machine. Drive.

-You ever wish for anything?

-Fresh rain.

-That sure doesn't sound like much of a wish.

-Yeah, well, I'm talkin rain with dancin' lightnin' and rollin' thunder.
The kinda rain that falls so hard and so fast that it washes the filth off
the roads. A clean hard fallin' rain that makes everythin' smell fresh.

94

-Do have to say you're a bright light.

-How's that?

-In all my days into nights you're one of the few I've come across that shine.

-Appreciate.

-Can I tell you my wish?

-Tell away.

-To be the breeze...that would be my wish. The breeze travels many roads...touches upon many things. To be the breeze.

-You too.

-What?

-Shine.

-Thanks.

-You betcha.

Long late afternoon shadows. A country mile northeast the ruins of a long ago forgotten town. Hawks circle in the deep blue of dusk

-The shadows are growing crowded up ahead.

-It really is somethin' the way the end of the day blue is streaked with red. Firin' beauty.

-Peace.

-Lost to a billion stars.

On this night he dreams of an old man from back when. Short worn man. Baggy black clothes. Floppy black beret. Bent crooked by the dumpster at the rear of the food store. Loads his shopping cart with loaves of stale bread. When he sees the old man he wants to ask if there's anything he can do for him. Always stops himself. I don't wanna cross the line. Then came a day when he sees the old man struggling with the cart. The front wheels are stuck on the cracked edge of a driveway. I cross the borderline. I'd never been so close. So old. Eyes watery red. A slight rattle and the wheels roll free. The old man's rawboned fingers reach out and touch my hand. He makes the sign of the cross. His soft voice, Live with yourself long enough and you will see.

Early morning weave of yellow-green swaying fields

    -Have you ever been lonely behind that drum worn wheel?
    -Naw. Bein' alone ain't the curse it's made out to be. Alone ain't
    lonely at least to the likes of an agin' soul like me.
    -You sure look to be on the satisfied side of life.
    -An ol' gospel has somethin' to do with that. As it's sung, When I've
    learned enough to really live, I'll be old enough to die. I just put my
    mind t'gatherin' all the life lessons here and now so I can do each day
    rightly on solid footin'.
    -Can I ask you something else?
    -Shoot.
    -What you said about old enough to die...
    -Not me, gospel song.
    -Yes. But, do you ever worry how much time you have left?
    -Time is takin' care of its own self. As it was framed on the T-shirts
    of the sixties, Today is the first day of the rest of my life.

In the lost rundown of getaways the sun sets behind clouds of red dust. The northern light disappears. A brilliant charge of lightning slices the black bordered sky.

    -Man O, man a heavy duty hard cleanin' rain is comin' to ol' 66.

-Wish come true.

-Ground 'em in the real and y'never know.

-The yellow road lines are flowing fast.1

-Movin' on.

-Never too late.

-Just let me know the way.

-Live the spirit.

-Findin' solitude of quiet dreamin'.

-Yes.

Clouds unmask a ghostly moon.

-Dreamin' on the drive or drivin' within a dream.

-Let the spirit live.

-Into the sacred night I go.

Golden-blue endless highway.

SHAKESPEARE & NIXON = HORROR SCREWED W/CRAZINESS

Deep into the night into the deep so far and long ago A duration of time I reach toward the black

ATTENHUT!

To the left To the left To the left right left

If I die in a combat zone Box me Sarge and send me home

My buddy Duke & me were out in the field 30 klicks south of DaNang heat rain banging A totally different no understanding world

HEAT RAIN BANGING

And there's Duke puttin' up a brave front for me, and me putting up a brave front for Duke and in between drags on our butts we are laughin' A funny strange kind of laughin' Cause if you ain't laughing You're gonna be crying

The black sky lights up like the 4th of July and like a thunder bolt it crashes at your ears You dig in Become a human mole There's no hidin' under the covers You're not safe at home You dig in Become that mole Breathe that dirt Those bugs And you pray for Life Pray for peace For another day Man who the hell would want another day of this But you want that Life Another Tomorrow

And then somehow, someway I could see folks marching down Main Street to the beat of the drum on Independence Day The stripes of America waving

Then God Bless it our fireworks cease Not even a whistle of air

Made it

That's when I would turn to Duke and Duke would turn to me

"Yeh man, fuckin-A we made IT!"

It was then in between drags on our butts and our funny strange kind of laughin' that we'd talk about this that and everything Here there and everywhere But mostly we talked about what we were going to do when we got out

"I'm gonna get a fiery red Harley-Davidson. And I'm gonna ride from coast to coast. In between. New Orleans. Get me some kicks on Route 66."

Duke he had more stable thoughts He was looking to be a marine biologist Commerce of the sea Regeneration of Life Of LIFE

Yeh in between drags on our butts and our funny strange kind of laughin' we'd talk about this that and everything Here there and everywhere

We even got around to RICHARD MILHOUSE NIXON

Duke was convinced Nixon was going to bring us home I was not holding my breath Yeh there Nixon is with Victory spread fingers

The end of 1969

40,024 dead

And there's Nixon with his fingers spread wide

    The end of 1970

    44,245 dead

    Victory?

    Sneaky panther games baby

    To the left To the left To the left right left If I die in a combat Zzzzzone

Bottom line we were all in it together Come together All together

Sinkin' deeper into that cloak of horror everyday Kill or be killed

And yeh we knew there were protesters back in the World didn't think we should be in the Nam But what did we know We just did what we were told

"Soldier."

"Yes Sir."

"Get a body count."

"Yes Sir."

And there we'd be countin' up the bodies Picking up parts of dead bodies A totally different no understanding world Yeh they forgot to remember back in the World that we were fighting for freedom Or were we trading freedom for CRAZINESS Cause there we are in the tangled limbs of the jungle sweatin' bullets

HEAT RAIN BANGING

"How all occasions do inform against me, And spur my dull revenge! What is a man, If his chief good and market of his time Be but to eat and feed? A beast, no more. Sure he that made us..."

He that made us? A beast no more And there's Duke laughin' his ass off Cause here we are in the tangled limbs of the jungle and I'm doin' HAMLET yeh, givin' Charlie an earful of Shakespeare baby Yeh man O man SHAKESPEARE hot&sweaty among the tangled limbs

"A beast, no more...Sure he that made us with such large discourse, Looking before and after, gave us not that capability and godlike reason To trust in us..."

God

Godlike reason

I'm out on patrol

"To be..."

Yeh

"Or not to be.."

Yeh yeh

"To be.."

Yeh

"Or not to be..."

Yeh yeh yeh

"To be, or not to be; that is the question."

BANG!

Yeh yeh

"To be, or not to be; that is the question."

BANG BANG BANG

Yeh yeh yeh

"Whether 'tis nobler in the mind to suffer The slings and arrows of outrageous fortune, Or to take arms against a sea of troubles, And by opposing end them. To die, to sleep -- "

In dying light Prez NIXON

"Give   me   the   laws   Give   me   the   troops   Give   me   the POWERRRRRRR!!"

"No Prez Man No Rain Peace"

At red dawn SHAKESPEARE

"To die, to sleep No more; and by a sleep to say we end The heart-ache, and the thousand natural shocks That flesh is heir to; 'tis a consummation Devoutly to be wished; to die, to sleep. To sleep? Perchance to dream."

ATTENHUT!

To the left To the left If I die in a combat zone

Box me Sarge and send home

CRAZINESS

Me and Duke are getting' short Knockin' them days off the calendar We are going back home Going back to the World

"I am going to get me that motorcycle. And I am going to ride from coast to coast. In between. New Orleans. Get me those kicks on Route 66. I am going to find me that two-lane blacktop of freedom. Ride away from all this CRAZINESS."

Duke writes a letter home to his folks tells them he doesn't mind being in the Nam as long as his little sister and brother have the same freedom he's had for the past 19 years

Then came that night when the darkness kicked up a storm of red&yellow light BANGING THUNDER at the ears Dig in Become that mole Breathe that dirt Those bugs Dig in This is it Had to be To be the end Figures lost on a vanishing landscape in the vicinity of Prez Nixon's VICTORY

CRASHING BANGING THUNDERING

I yelled "Quiet" once Yelled "Quiet" twice

And there came a coffin of silence The rockets stopped bursting in air As fast as the attack came it ended Man O man Made it! It was then that I'd turn to Duke and Duke would turn to me.

"Yeh, man, fuckin'-A we..."

Duke wasn't there Not there Took a direct hit from enemy rocket fire

Duke was just a few yards away   Now gone   Duke was my buddy   A brother   Always there Now no more The eruption of agony screamed in Heart & Mind   A soul gone from the landscape

Duke's flag covered coffin came to rest under the soil of Arlington National Cemetery.   Quiet forever.

11 years later November 13, 1982 the Vietnam War Memorial is dedicated in Washington, D.C.   Family and friends are reflected in the mirror-like surface of the Black Wall as they leave tokens of remembrance. Tracings of names are taken from the Wall.   So many names from all parts of these United States.

58,022.

I'm at the east end of the Wall panel 55

My hand is shaking as my eyes

count down the names to line 22

I see the letters that form his name

I reach towards the black

"We made it."

In strange kind of way we had made it.

102

Cause on that November day I was able to reach out to Duke once again on U.S. soil

        FINGERS ACROSS THE LETTERS

        LETTERS THAT MAKE UP A NAME

        ON THE SHINY BLACK WALL

WOMAN & MAN

"Good coffee."

"Yeah."

"Good and hot."

"Yeah."

"You seem..."

"What?"

"You seem...I don't know...happy."

"Happy?"

"Yes. I mean more than usual."

"Oh?"

"You have a nice smile."

"Yeah?"

"Did something...happen?"

"Happen?"

"Yes."

"No...not really."

"Not really?"

"Well..."

"What?"

"Nothing really."

"No, something happened."

"Yeah...well..."

"Are you going to tell me?"

"It's just..."

"What?"

"Well..."

"What? Come on."

"I wrote about what happened Saturday...today."

"About what happened..."

"Saturday."

"Saturday?"

"I wrote about it today."

"Today? You're not being clear."

"I wrote about what happened Saturday. Today."

"Wrote...about what?"

"You know..."

"No, I...you don't mean...?"

"Yeah."

"You wrote.."

"Yeah."

"About that?"

"Yeah."

"How do you mean...you wrote about it?

"In my journal."

"Your...?"

"I wrote about it."

"You keep a journal?"

"Yeah."

"And you wrote about what happened Saturday...today?"

"Yeah."

"That was private. You wrote about our private life in a journal?"

"Yeah."

"When did you start keeping a journal?"

"A while back."

"Have you written other things about us?"

"Yeah."

"Private things?"

"Yeah."

"You didn't, not really."

"Really."

"And you wrote about last Saturday…"

"Today."

"You wrote about when we went…downstairs?"

"It was dark."

"Very."

'Yeah."

"And you wrote about when we went into that room?"

"Yeah."

"And how you put your lips…"

"Yeah."

"And your fingers…"

"Yeah."

"And then how I…"

"Yeah."

"And how we…"

"Yeah."

"You wrote about all that?"

"I did…yeah."

"I'm surprised."

"Yeah?"

"Yes…I'm quite surprised."

"Really?"

"Yes…you…surprise me."

"I thought…"

"What?"

"You'd be…"

"Be what?"

"Pleased."

"Pleased?"

"Yeah."

"I didn't say I wasn't pleased."

"Oh?"

"Surprised?"

"Are you?"

"What?"

"Pleased. I thought…"

"What?"

"That you'd be flattered."

"Flattered?"

"And pleased."

"I am. Flattered and pleased."

"But surprised?"

"Yes, surprised."

"Why?"

"I didn't know that you…"

"What?"

"Wrote. And about that."

"Yeah."

"Us."

"Yeah."

"Did you write about afterwards when we…"

"Yeah."

"And then how I put my..."

"Yeah."

"And how you put your..."

"Yeah."

"And how I..."

"Yeah."

"You wrote about all that?"

"I did...yeah."

"That's beautiful."

"Yeah?"

"Yes. That you can express yourself so well."

"Yeah."

"To be so articulate is a gift."

"Well..."

"You should feel proud."

"Proud."

"Yes."

"Well..."

"You write..."

"Yeah."

"And about...that."

"Yeah."

"Did you...have you...written about other times when we..."

"Yeah."

"This must be a big journal."

"Very."

"We had some good times."

"Many."

"And you wrote about all...all the times we..."

"Not all."

"Just some?"

"Yeah."

"Why just some?"

"The best times."

"I thought they were all the best."

"Yeah...but...well, you know..."

"They weren't all the best for you?"

'Yeah, but..."

"I'm surprised."

"Surprised?"

"That you don't think...well...that every time was the best."

"Very good."

"But not good enough to write about?"

"Selective. The more textured times."

"Textured?"

"You know."

"No."

"Like the time on the..."

"What?"

"The sink."

"The sink?"

"The bathroom in the L-shaped apartment."

"Yes."

"And the kitchen..."

"The wood block table."

"You were up..."

"Yes."

"And I was..."

"Yes."

"And we were..."

"Yes...Yes..."

"Textured."

"Yes, textured."

"That's it."

"A textured...time."

"Yeah."

"Like the time in the car."

"Car?"

"By that abandoned building in the woods."

"Yeah."

"And on the summer grass..."

"Yeah."

"...under the shade tree..."

"Yeah."

"...by the river."

"Yeah."

"Textured, huh?"

"It's all how you frame it."

"You're scary."

"Me?"

"Textured."

"It's all in the doing."

"Doing?"

"Yes. The doing. The space and time of it. You. Me. Woman. Man. We are the texture of it. I write about our love. What we share."

"The time of it."

"Yeah."

"The being."

"Yeah."

"You and me."

"Our life. You're the part of life that makes it all worthwhile. I glory in you."

"Thank you."

"I mean everything…"

"I know."

"Every word."

"I wrote something too. Not about any special time, place or date. Just something I wrote. I would like for you to read it."

"This is written by you?"

"Yes. Read it out loud."

"No."

"No?"

"It's for you to read…so I can hear."

"No, I…"

"Yeah."

"I wrote it understand…just wrote it…thinking of you. Us."

"We."

"Him to me. Lips to lips. Hands in mine. Our bodies together. Held with his eyes in mine. Him to me. Me to him. We."

"Us."

"This is good…coffee."

"Would you like another cup?"

"No, thank you. I think we should leave…go someplace."

"Someplace?"

"Yes. Someplace. Perhaps we can find something…textured for you to write about."

"Us."

"What?"

"For us...to write about."

"Yes."

"Yeah."

GRANNY

beautiful day, picked some daisies,

packed up a few beers.

rode over the MT to talk w/Granny.

i did the talking, seeing that i was doin' the drinkin'.

talked about this, that & everything

under the crystal blue.

words always came easy w/the Granny.

w/a few oz's left

i straightened the daisies on Granny's grave.

then gave the sun-streaked grass

a taste of the brew.

Granny did like her beer.

yeh, indeed.

as i walked away i saw a pretty little girl

who appeared out of nowhere looking to the sky

What are you looking at?

I'm seeing all the folks that are

resting here. Rocking away on their

porches in the clouds.

i knew Granny heard & smiled.

About the Author

Sean Michael Rice was a humbled soul who lived in Pennsylvania.